Life with Brody

A findmysoulmate.org Book

K. F. Johnson

WESTBOW
PRESS®
A DIVISION OF THOMAS NELSON
& ZONDERVAN

WestBow Press books may be ordered through booksellers or by contacting:

WestBow Press
A Division of Thomas Nelson & Zondervan
1663 Liberty Drive
Bloomington, IN 47403
www.westbowpress.com
1 (866) 928-1240

Scripture taken from the New King James Version®. Copyright © 1982 by Thomas Nelson. Used by permission. All rights reserved.

ISBN: 978-1-9736-7367-5 (sc)
ISBN: 978-1-9736-7368-2 (hc)
ISBN: 978-1-9736-7366-8 (e)

Library of Congress Control Number: 2019914053

Print information available on the last page.

WestBow Press rev. date: 10/09/2019

Acknowledgements

I would like to thank my friends, Cheryl Mallory, Kim Johnson and Beth MacGregor, for advice on medical and physical therapy points. Thank you to Maleah McCulley and Janet Bly for editing help. My friend Tina, thank you for being there through thick and thin. For the support of all my children, you have inspired and encouraged me. And to my husband, Greg. Thank you for believing in me from the very beginning. I am blessed.

Prologue

I was sitting with my feet up on the couch, watching TV with my husband, Steve, who was kicked back in his recliner. One of those findmysoulmate.org commercials came on, and Steve casually said, "I wonder if *we* signed up, if they would make us a match."

"I don't know," I replied. And gave it no more thought.

Three months later, I sat there at my computer contemplating my decision. I was about to hit *send* on my profile. I can't tell you why I was doing it. It felt like our love had gone cold. That statement Steve made kept rolling through my head.

Are we really compatible? Is that why we seem to just exist together?

We used to be partners. Not anymore. Everything seemed so different. For the past several months, longer to be honest, we seemed more like roommates. We were supposed to be 'helpmeets' for life. That's God's plan. But we weren't living it. I couldn't get him to go to church with me. People wondered where my husband was. I hated going alone, but I knew that I would hate not going even more. So, why would I fill out that profile? Simple. I was curious. It was cheating, and I knew it. I was curious, true, but *this* curiosity could lead to real trouble and possibly end my marriage. What was I thinking?

… send…

1

It had been two weeks since I set up my account on that dating site, and I hadn't checked my profile. I didn't want to see it. *What if someone replied? What if no one replied? Maybe I should delete it. That would be the best thing, right? Yeah, that's what I'll do. I'll go in and delete it. That's all.*

Wow, forty-five replies! I looked at their pictures—my age range and good looking. They were doing things that looked fun to me. I'd love to go boating, hiking, snorkeling, or horseback riding. Well, maybe not snorkeling; I'm too far from the ocean. Oh, look, this guy said he likes picnics after church. What a nice smile. *I won't delete anyone yet. It won't hurt to look. Wouldn't it be funny if Steve put his name in here, and I saw him? I wonder if that's why he mentioned it.*

By the time I checked through all forty-five replies, I had found some interesting men. I deleted all but five. Steve wasn't one of them. Did that mean he signed up, but we weren't compatible? Did he just make a comment, wondering aloud, not really intending to do it? So like him.

He always talked about stuff he never did. How many times had he said he would fix the faucet or the door, and it didn't get done? He said for a week he was going to mow the lawn, and guess who actually did it? Yep, me. Like always. He always told me he was *going to* do something for me or with me, but it never happened. *I'm not important to him anymore. Maybe I never was.*

Oh God, what should I do? Well, that was a stupid question. I should get off here and not entertain this idea at all. But I was so tired of being in a loveless marriage. I was lonely and alone, even when he was in the room with me. What harm would it be if I just responded to these five? Seriously, I could stop at any time. I didn't have to meet them; it wasn't like that. What was the harm in having a friend? I should be allowed friends too. Seemed like all I did was work and come home. I went to the grocery store and to church, but that was it. *Steve goes fishing with his buddies. They get together to watch sports. The irony is that I like football too. I often sit home and watch the games after he leaves, but he never talks to me about them. He never asked me if I want to go with him. That would be nice. I would love that.*

I tried talking to him about football once. It did me no good. He said, "Seriously, April, do you even understand the game?" How rude was that? It couldn't have hurt worse if he'd slapped me in the face. *So what if I don't understand all the rules? I may not know the difference between a nickel back and a halfback, but I am willing to learn. Why can't he teach me? We talked about all kinds of things when we dated. That seems like a lifetime ago.*

Our seven-year anniversary is next month. Is this the seven-year itch? I wish I knew. Is he as unhappy as I am?

I was afraid to ask such a loaded question. A yes or a no could start a fight, and I don't like conflict. *This is so hard. I want a better marriage, but I don't know how to go about it. God help me.*

I DECIDED TO TALK TO Steve. When I got home from work, I made one of his favorite dinners: hamburger steaks, mashed potatoes, gravy, and French-style green beans. I had everything ready and waiting at six o'clock, our regular dinnertime. Guess what? Yep, no show! I waited until six thirty before I decided to eat alone.

Steve arrived at seven thirty-five with no phone call and no explanation. "Hey, babe. Sorry I'm late. What smells so good?" I recited the menu for him as he washed up at the sink. "Sounds good," he replied as he dished up. "I'm starving and tired. Crazy day."

He ate his supper with little conversation, told me thanks with a kiss on the top of my head, hit the shower, and went to bed. I wondered if he was having an affair. *Could that be it? Could he be cheating on me? Oh, God, no! I couldn't handle that. I'm so stupid.*

I bet that is it. That is why he mentioned the dating website. He wanted me to look for someone else because he already had someone. I thought I was going to be sick. I didn't want to jump to conclusions, but what was I supposed to think? *Should I check his phone?* That would be too sneaky. I refused to do that or be that kind of person.

I'll try again tomorrow night. That's it. I can't give up on him. Not yet. I love him. I do. Maybe we are too comfortable together. It was like we don't have to talk anymore. How sad is that?

SECOND TRY AT A SECOND chance. I had on a cute little blue dress that I wore to work. I hoped to capture his eye as well. I made another of Steve's favorite dinners. Tonight was oven-fried chicken and baked potatoes with corn and biscuits. He came home right on time.

"Hey, April," he said. "What smells so good?"

"Winner, winner chicken dinner," I replied, doing the Vanna White wave toward the food, "with all the fixings."

"Oh." There was disappointment in his voice. "I had chicken for lunch. Some of us went out to discuss plans about the new section."

Deflated, I said, "I'm sorry, I didn't know. Did you have a good day?"

"Yeah," he said. "We got the new section to this complex figured out, and it's all a go."

"Well, that's good." I gathered my courage and asked, "You have any plans this weekend? Maybe we could do something together."

We sat down, and I silently said a prayer while Steve waited to dish up. *An improvement*, I thought. *He used to plow right through.*

He picked up the thread of conversation. "Sorry, babe, the guys and I are going to the lake to camp and fish."

I was hurt, but I tried to sound casual. "Sounds like fun." I hoped he would invite me along.

"Yeah, it should be. I'll leave early Friday and get back Sunday afternoon, before dinner. I'll be hungry, I'm sure. And tired too, most likely. Camping is fun, but it wears on you."

I wondered, *Do the other guys bring their wives?* I braved myself to ask him. "Who's all going this weekend?"

"You know, the usual crowd."

What did that mean? I didn't know who "the usual crowd" was, but it didn't include me. I was done with this conversation. We finished our meal in silence, and I struggled to control my emotions and get my food down.

It's Friday night, *and I am home alone again. I am so tired of this. I'm not his wife; I'm his housekeeper and cook.* I kept wondering if our lives would be different if we had kids. *But right now, I'm*

glad we don't. I'd hate to drag kids through a divorce. Wow! Am I really thinking divorce?

I decided to spend time on the computer. I balanced the checkbook, paid bills, and worked on research for my job. Then I visited the dating site. *What's the harm? It's not like I'm in a real marriage any way.*

Bob three-five-seven sent me a message. Mr. "Picnic after Church" reached out to me. How nice is that?

A251, this is Bob357. I wanted to introduce myself and get to know a little more about you. Then we could go from there. How does that sound? I'm thirty-seven years old. I'm a professional, and I've been at the same job for over a decade. That makes me either stable or boring. I enjoy hiking, camping, and fishing. I love the outdoors. I go to church every Sunday and on Wednesday night, work permitting. My relationship with my Savior is very important to me, and I don't want to be involved with anyone who doesn't know Jesus too. Are you a Christian?

Bob357, this is A251. Yes, I do love Jesus. I also go to church twice a week. I grew up in a Christian home but never came to Jesus myself until a few years ago. I agree; it's not good to be in a relationship with someone who doesn't share your faith. The Bible tells us not to be unequally yoked. I'm twenty-eight years old. I haven't hiked in forever, so I don't know if I would enjoy that anymore. But I've never gone camping. I am used to my creature comforts! I would love to learn to fish though. I like to eat fish, so that's the next logical step, right? I am also a professional. I've been in the same job, same company since graduating college. So if stable and reliable are boring, that makes two of us! I would like to get a dog. Do you like animals? I'm sorry to be jumping subjects on you. I'm just throwing thoughts out. Talk to you later.

2

I got up early, ate breakfast, and showered before I checked around the house. *Where could I put a dog bed? Where would I put the food dish? So many things to consider when adding a new household member.* I dressed comfortably and casually, and I headed out the door.

At ten o'clock, I was outside the animal shelter, excited and waiting for the doors to open. It had been a long time since I was excited about anything.

I introduced myself to the woman behind the counter. She was a short, plump, middle-aged woman with a sweet smile. "I am looking for a dog," I chattered nervously. "I haven't had a pet in years. Not since I was a kid in my parents' house. I'm hoping you have a dog that can put up with a newbie."

The lady smiled at me with humor in her eyes, "Well, April, that's what we do here. We put people and animals together to make good forever homes. Let me show you what we have."

"Great. Doesn't matter to me, large or small. I want one that will fit my work schedule and personality. I do have a big fenced backyard, but I work five days a week, so it would have to be okay being alone during the day. I'm sure I can get a dog door installed."

She took me to a big kennel area. She dragged her right

hand across the fence covering the dog run. "These are the puppies, but I don't think that would be a good idea for you. You need a more mature dog, already housebroke."

"Sounds good," I said.

"Okay." She pointed to her left. "This section has older dogs. They will have some training, but you would still need to walk them and work with them. Any dog is going to take time and attention."

"I understand. I was thinking of nice morning walks, bike rides, that kind of stuff." I pointed to a medium-sized black and white dog. "Tell me about this one."

"This is Mickey." She looked over his kennel cover sheet. "He's a border collie mix. He would love the active stuff you mentioned. Border collies are a working breed, so activity is good."

We moved down to the next kennel. "This one here is Brody," she said, indicating a long-haired dog with red/liver-colored hair. He had a white chest and white paws and amber eyes. "He's a mix. We're figuring German shepherd, Australian shepherd, and a little something else. Another active dog and a good companion for hiking or watching a movie. And then there's this guy." A handsome black dog with a white mark on his chest came over to the gate as we approached. "His name is Bobby. He's a Lab mix. He would love walks, maybe some swimming, and he'd be a good snuggler. You have to be careful about letting any of these guys on your bed though. They're big enough to take over!"

I smiled. "Can I meet them all? You know, one at a time, to see how we click? I want to get this right."

"Perfect. We can take them one at a time into the training room."

I spent the next two hours meeting and playing with each

dog. I asked a lot of questions. I had a long form to fill out. I think I spent less time doing the paperwork for my house loan, but like the lady said, they needed to make sure I'd be a good dog owner and the dog was going to a good home—hopefully their forever home. I got approved, paid my fee, and led Brody out the door. I loaded him in the back seat of my SUV and put the windows halfway down so he could do the "happy dog with his head out the window" thing. He loved it. He looked very happy as we pulled out of the parking lot. I know I was smiling, big-time.

"WELL, BRODY," I SAID, PATTING him as we stood in the parking lot, "this is a pet store. Dogs get to go in here, but not all stores will let you in."

Brody looked up at me with his soulful eyes and seemed to understand.

"Let's go pick out your new bed, get you some food, and who knows what else. I'm sure you are as expensive as a kid. I'm glad the shelter gave me some coupons."

Brody and I wandered around the store for over an hour. We looked at beds, food, treats, collars, dishes, and toys. I grabbed squeaky toys, tennis balls, and tug-of-war ropes and showed them all to Brody. He seemed excited about everything, so I grabbed a variety and headed over to the dog doors. There were some you could install in your own back door, but that required cutting the door. I looked at the size I would need for Brody. A person could easily fit though the hole. I didn't like that idea at all.

A salesperson showed me one that was a panel for the sliding glass door. That seemed easier and felt safer, so that's what I got. I also got a dog tag that said "Brody" on one side, and the other side read "April & Steve" with our phone number and hometown. The microchips would only work if someone checked for it. A tag with our name and number was an instant contact, which I hoped I would never need.

"Wow," I told Brody as we drove away, "I was right. You are as expensive as a child, but I hope all this stuff will help you feel at home." I turned onto our street and pointed out our house. "Here it is: your new home. Let's go! I hope the installation video on this dog door is as easy as the clerk said it would be."

Brody entered our split-level home and, instinctively, headed up stairs. I put the bags on the dining room table before I showed him around the house. I put his dog bed in the corner of the living room. He plopped down on it, but he got up quickly when I left the room. I took him downstairs and showed him the laundry room, guest room, and den. We headed out the door under the large deck into the backyard. He took off and started checking out *his* yard. I double-checked the fence as he explored. I hadn't thought about it when we first moved in, but now that this yard held a dog, the fence was important. I left Brody in the backyard while I finished unloading the car. He stayed close by me while I worked on getting the panel with the dog door set up in the sliding glass door. "Okay, Brody," I announced, throwing my arms around his neck, "you're home!"

I made myself a little dinner and sat down at the table with my phone in hand. My mom answered on the third ring.

"Hello?"

"Hey, Mom, how are you?"

"April, good, to hear your voice, as always. What's new?"

"Oh, about seventy-five pounds of fluff and fur on four paws."

"Excuse me? April, did you get a dog?"

"I knew you'd be shocked. But you have to meet him, Mom.

He's so cool, and he has these soulful amber eyes that melt right into your heart."

My mother's laughter sounded like a song, and it made me smile. We talked for the better part of an hour about Brody, work, and my sister, June. Yes, we were both named for the months we were born in. Nothing too original there, I know. I was always glad I wasn't born in October or February.

SUNDAY AFTERNOON, WHILE I WAS getting dinner ready, I heard Steve pull in. "Well, Brody, here he comes. Time to meet your new dad."

He looked at me and cocked his head.

Steve called out, "April, I'm home!"

Bark, bark, bark!

"April?" The question in his voice made me grin.

Brody lumbered over to the top of the living room stairs, wagging his stubby tail.

"Steve, meet Brody."

"Hi, Brody." Steve bent over, patting and scratching him. "Who does he belong to?"

"Well, dear," I said, "he's ours. I got him this weekend."

"What? You got a dog? I thought you didn't like dogs."

"I never said I didn't like dogs."

"Yes, you did," he said. "When you met my mother's dog. You said it was a horrible little creature."

"Well, dear," I said as sweetly as I could, "that's because it is spoiled beyond reason, its breath smells like poop, and it's a six-pound ball of fur. It's a mop without a handle. I love dogs—just not that one."

Steve threw back his head and let out a full-blown laugh.

It made my heart sing. *That's the man I fell in love with. When he smiles and laughs like that, he makes me feel alive. Thanks, Brody!*

"So," he asked, "what smells so good?"

"Pork chops with all the fixings. Ready to eat?"

He rubbed his belly. "I'm starving. We spent more time working on Richard's boat than fishing. I think it's true what they say, BOAT stands for 'break out another thousand.'"

"Cute. I hadn't heard that one before. Who's Richard?"

"The new foreman on this project." He headed for the table with a couple of plates. "Nice guy. He lives close by the lake so he invited a bunch of us from work for a guys' weekend. He says with a wife and four teenage girls, he needs some time away from all the hormones."

"I can see why he would need to escape now and then." I followed him to the table with silverware and glasses. "If he ever does family time, maybe the three of us could go."

"What? You would go camping and fishing?"

"Well, I'd be willing to try. I haven't camped since I was a kid, but if I could sleep comfortably, I think I'd be okay. I've never fished, but I like to eat them. Might be fun to learn."

Steve threw back his head and laughed again. He called Brody over. Brody hurried right over. Steve patted his side. "Thanks, Brody. I think you might help make my lovely wife an outdoorsy person."

In the morning, Steve gave me a kiss on his way out the door and wished me a good day. I don't know who enjoyed our morning walk more—me or Brody. It felt like the start of something good. Or should I say a *restart*?

Thank you, Jesus!

Brody did well on the leash, and I sure enjoyed the fresh morning air. A great way to begin the day.

I CALLED THE VET AND made an appointment for Brody on Thursday afternoon. I left work early that day, picked him up, and away we went. He enjoyed the car ride. We parked at the vet's office. I let Brody out of the car to sniff around and check things out. He was a happy dog checking out all the scents in the area. I opened the door to the office. End of happy dog. He pulled back, sat down, and sprawled out on the ground.

One of the staff members saw our struggle and offered him a dog treat. Bribery got us through the door, but as soon as the escape door closed, Brody looked at me like I had betrayed him. Maybe it was the smells. Maybe something about the office reminded him of the shelter.

I held in my laughter as I approached the front desk. "Appointment for Brody."

They weighed him. The vet checked him and put a microchip in his back between his shoulder blades. He got his shots, and we were good to go. Brody left the exam room with his tail tucked and his head down. I felt for him, but it had to be done. Next, we were off to city hall to get his tags so he could be legal around the neighborhood and at the local parks.

Back in the car, I said, "All set, Brody. You're legal now and officially part of our family. Look, the bill even says 'Brody MacIntyre.' How cool is that?" He barely raised an eyebrow.

DURING THE NEXT WEEK, STEVE and I seemed to engage in conversation more and were more at ease around each other. It felt like we were getting back to where we used to be.

Saturday morning, I got up early and took Brody for our walk. I was sitting on the deck afterward reading my Bible. Brody was busy in the backyard. I saw Steve standing at the sliding glass door and checking out the dog door. I waved, put my Bible down on the table beside me, and just watched Brody for a while. I was deep in thought when Steve joined me on the deck.

"Good morning." He leaned over and kissed my cheek. "You did a good thing there, April." He gestured to Brody. "He's a good dog. I'm glad you rescued him."

I smiled. "Thank you. I'm glad too. I think he's happy here."

"Yeah. The dog door, that's a pretty clever idea."

"I thought so. If we are all gone, we can take it out, and no one will get in the house. And Brody has access to the backyard when he's here alone."

Steve nodded. "You're right. This is safer. Clever, very clever.

"Hey, why don't we take Brody for a hike? There's a spot not far from where we camped last weekend with some nice trails. I bet he would like it. How about it?"

Wow! My heart about jumped, but I didn't want to seem *too* eager. "I would love that. And our boy out there would be in heaven."

"Good. I have a few things to do first. Let's take off at ten, get in a hike, and head somewhere for lunch. We'll still beat the heat."

"Sounds good to me. We'll be ready," I replied.

Neither of us moved right away as we sat and relaxed in the silence for a few minutes. We watched Brody just being a dog in his yard. Once again, I felt thankful for Brody bringing my husband back to me. Then it hit me. *Getting this dog was God's plan. Could it be this simple?*

Time to go. Brody sat on his bed in the living room and watched as we got things together. When I put his leash by the door, he came right over. It made me smile. Steve stood by the dining room table and studied us with a look of contentment on his face. At least, that's what I hoped I saw there.

We had an enjoyable hike, gorgeous scenery, and good conversation. Brody rode in the back seat, his head out the window, mouth open, ears flapping in the breeze.

I looked over at Steve, and he grabbed my hand.

"I wonder why he was put up for adoption," I said. "I can't find a thing wrong with him."

"Maybe someone had to move and couldn't bring him," Steve offered. "Or the owner got sick. Not all rescue dogs are abused."

"I'm just curious about his story."

"They say dogs live in the now," Steve commented. "They forgive and move on. People should be more like that."

"That's what Jesus says too," I replied.

"What?"

"That's what Jesus talks about. He says if we ask Him for forgiveness, He not only forgives our sins but they are forgotten. They are removed as far as the east is from the west."

"Maybe some things are unforgivable," Steve snapped.

I wondered at Steve's abrupt response. "Just think about the way Brody loved us. Immediate and complete. Jesus is that way too."

I could see the muscles in Steve's jaw clench. I hit a nerve.

"We're here. The trailhead is at the end of the parking lot. It's not a long hike, but we can go to the top of that ridge. We'll be able to see over the lake. The views are great."

"I'm glad I packed my camera," I said, reaching for my bag. "Let's let Brody go off leash, okay?"

"Other hikers might come along with their dogs. Until we know him better and know how he is with other dogs, we better keep him on the leash."

"Okay," I said.

Soon, we were off. The trail was an easy, but steady climb. Brody was busy checking everything out. Everything was new to him. I don't know what was busier: his nose or his little snub of a tail.

When we met some other hikers with a yellow Lab, Brody behaved himself.

An hour later, we reached the top. The view was worth the hike. The trail continued but we stayed there. I loved it. Steve and I were spending time together—all because of Brody.

We gave Brody some free time. I grabbed my camera and grabbed a few shots. Pictures of Brody playing and running around. Pictures of Steve relaxing. And, of course, incredible scenery shots. We chatted with other hikers who passed by, and many said it was their favorite hike. It was easy to see why.

When it was time to go, we all got a drink of water before heading down the mountain. We put Brody back on his leash, and off we went. The trip back went a bit faster. Before I knew it, we were back in the car.

"Thank you." I squeezed Steve's hand. "Such a perfect day."

He looked me in the eye and responded, "What made you decide to get Brody?"

I took a deep breath. "I didn't want to be alone, and I thought he could keep me company." *There, I said it. I didn't mean to hurt him, but that was the truth.*

"Where would you like to go to lunch?" he said, avoiding the subject.

"I don't care really, but I don't want to leave Brody in the car too long. He might get overheated pretty fast."

"Good point. How about a drive-through and eat at the park? We can sit at the picnic tables with Brody."

"Sounds good to me." I buckled myself in.

So, that's what we did. We ordered burgers, including one for Brody without the bun, and we drove to Memorial Park. It was a few blocks from our house. Lots of trees, picnic tables at one end, and playground equipment at the other, the kind with big tube slides and wooden forts. A pretty little stream along one side. A large, open grassy area, water fountains, and grills. Families everywhere, including ours, the three of us. I felt like we were dating again. We found a covered picnic table by a tree and ate our lunch. We set out a dish of water for Brody and gave him his burger. He devoured his treat, settled down close by us, and took a nap.

OUR DRIVE HOME WAS QUIET and calm, both of us lost in our thoughts, until Brody let out stinky dog farts. We looked at each other, snickered, and then groaned.

"I think the burger was a bad idea," I said as I opened my window.

Steve cranked opened his window too and said, "He looks proud of himself, the little stinker." Laughter ensued again.

When we got home and unloaded, Brody went straight to the backyard, then came in, stretched out on his bed, and went to sleep.

"I think we wore him out," Steve said.

"Me too. I'm tired and sore too, but it's a good tired." I slipped off my shoes and put my feet up on the coffee table.

"So, what now?" he asked.

"I have some housework to do. What about you?"

"Yeah, I've got stuff to do. What are you doing tomorrow?" He stopped by the end of the couch.

"Before or after church?" I asked.

"I should've known," he replied tersely.

"You are welcome to join me. I would love that."

"No, I'm busy." He turned and walked away.

The magic left with him. Something literally seemed to deflate with his exit. It hurt my heart.

3

Sunday morning, I took Brody for a walk before church. Steve had still been in bed when I took my shower. When I got done, he was on the deck, watching Brody in the yard, and he seemed to be lost in thought. I joined him on the deck and asked again if he'd like to join me at church. He declined. I gave him a kiss goodbye and headed out the door.

Mom met me at church. She lived in the town just to the west of us. My sister, June, and her husband, Larry, lived in the town just to the west of that. Mom went to church with me once a month. She did the same with June and Larry. We were a close family, but we didn't live in each other's pockets.

After a good service, a good sermon, and good fellowship, I got home and discovered Steve was gone. No note. Just gone. I did some housework and sat down at my computer. I thought I'd tell Bob357 I got a dog, but first I deleted the four other guys who had responded. Talking to one guy was enough.

"Hello, A251. Good to hear from you. First of all, I'm glad to hear you're a Christian. Yes, I like animals. I have a dog. He's my partner and friend. His name is Bo. I don't know what I'd do without him. We go everywhere together. I think he's part of what keeps me active."

"Bob 357, good to hear from you again. I got a dog. I went

to the local shelter and rescued a shepherd mix. Not too large, but big and active enough to keep me going. His name is Brody. We've been going for walks all week, and yesterday we went on a hike—my first in ages. Brody loved it. His first significant outing; it was a real test. We both passed."

Send.

Oh, my goodness, what am I doing? I only considered Bob357 as a friend, but this is a dating site. I should not be doing this.

Exit.

Power down.

I got up from my desk and left the room, arguing with myself. *Okay, that's it. I'm not going back on there. I'm not. Except to close my account. But I'm definitely not going back on today.*

I got busy looking for something to make for dinner and wondered where my husband was. It bothered me that I didn't know, but I knew I had to trust him, and mostly, trust God. Sometimes that's easier to say than it is to live. I kept thinking I should confront him about the affair suspicion.

But what if I'm wrong? He would be hurt. And if I'm right, my marriage could end right then and there. How can I be so brave on one point and so weak on another? I'm an intelligent person. I have a degree in accounting, and I was one of the top five people in my graduating class. So brave and so foolish all wrapped into one huge mess. Only God could love such a wretch. Thank you, Lord.

I WAS JUST FINISHING DINNER when Steve came home. Brody ran to greet him. They say that dogs are a good judge of character, and Brody loved Steve from the start. Steve captured my heart right away too. What had happened to us? Things did seem to be improving in some areas. *I should be grateful for that.*

"Hey, babe." I greeted him with a smile. "How are you?"

"Okay. Something smells good." He walked over to the stove.

"Meatloaf, baked potatoes, and salad." I grabbed the salad bowls and dinner plates from the cupboard.

He gave Brody another pat and headed off to wash up. As I watched him go, I prayed for him—and for me: *God, please help me to be the wife and friend he needs me to be. Help me, Lord, to not be a stumbling block, but a reflection of You in all I say and do. Please open my husband's heart and mind to receive You. Amen.*

At dinner, Steve seemed preoccupied at first, but then we began a conversation about his building project. I am so fascinated by the construction world—to be able to drive by a building and know my husband had a hand in building that is cool. I can only imagine how it must feel for him to drive through an area and point out, "I built that and that."

"Did you know Jesus was a carpenter?" I asked.

"I did. There's a guy on the job with a bumper sticker that says 'My boss is a Jewish carpenter.' I asked him about it one day. We talked about Jesus for a few minutes. He told me about all the controversy too. About Mary being pregnant when they got married."

God, help me to handle this right. My non-believing husband is talking about You!

"Yeah," I said. "Right from the start. People knew Mary was pregnant when she married Joseph. The neighbors did the math when Jesus was born and knew He was created out of wedlock. It may not seem like a big deal nowadays, but back then, it was huge. Must have been very hard for both His folks. But I've got to give major kudos to Joseph for stepping up to the plate."

"What do you mean?" He sounded curious.

"Well, he knew it wasn't his baby. An angel came to him in

a dream and told him the baby was God's. He took it on faith and chose to be a good dad to Jesus. Not everyone can be a stepparent. Some people try and fail miserably. Imagine being the stepfather to the Lord. That had to be hard."

Steve continued to eat in silence.

After I while I added, "Joseph taught Jesus about carpentry, like a good dad should."

"You talk like you know these people," he commented.

"I feel like I do—through the stories in the Bible."

"You *really* believe all that stuff, don't you?" he asked.

"Of course, I do. It's the truth," I explained. "People have tried to prove the Bible wrong. They end up proving it to be true. Matter of fact, most all who have tried to refute it end up becoming believers."

"So," he asked, "why is it so important to you?"

"What, the Bible?" I asked.

"Yeah. Why is it so important to you?"

I said a quick prayer before I answered. "Because the Bible is the Word of God. It's where I learn about Him, about what happened in the past, and about what's coming in the future. It's my daily guide to life."

"What?" There was a look of confusion on his face. "You mean you read about the future in it?"

"Not like you mean. It's not the *Farmer's Almanac* where you check out what the weather's going to be like next spring, but it does tell us about how and when things will end. But 'no man shall know the day and the hour,' it's not specific like that. Otherwise, some people would live their lives in debauchery and sin until two weeks before the end and then turn their lives over to God."

"It's like a how-to book then. You read it so you know what to do every day?"

"Yes and no. It will tell you how to handle different situations in life because there are examples in it. It certainly tells me how to be a better person."

"Well," he said, "you're a better person than I am."

"No, believe me," I argued, "I make my share of mistakes. The thing is, I know I am forgiven."

That was the most Steve and I had talked about Jesus since I became a Christian three years before. I tried at the time to share my faith with him, but it seemed to drive him away.

Come to think of it, that was the start of our struggles. The devil seemed to get his dander up and fought hard against us. *It feels like I just woke up and realized what a mess I made of everything. Have I been driving my husband away? Is it too late to get him back? Lord, please, help me. Please protect our marriage and our love.*

4

It's Thursday night, and Steve's late coming home again. I decided to go online and delete my account. However, I didn't realize more people had responded to me. It took me a while, but I finally figured out how to mark my account so I wouldn't get any new contacts. Then, I deleted everyone but Bob357. *Next step is to tell Bob357 that I'm signing off.*

"A251, how exciting to hear about Brody. I'm glad you've got some company for yourself and that you went hiking. A friend of mine offers fishing classes. I bet they have that kind of stuff in your area. Check out the newspaper ads. Better not bring the dog though. You'll need to concentrate on fishing."

"Thanks, Bob357. I didn't know people taught fishing. That's hilarious! Sounds like a good idea though. I'll check it out and let you know what happens."

Send.

Oops, I forgot to tell him I was deleting my account. But how could I do that to someone who sounded so nice? Besides, we're just friends. No mention of romance by either of us. Of course, I haven't told him I'm married either. I'm scum.

I grabbed the paper. Sure enough, a guy was offering fishing classes the next three weekends. *What would Steve think of that?* I decided I was going to ask him when he got home.

Or not.

I ate my dinner and cleaned up after myself. Steve's food was on the counter, cold, when he pulled in at eight-thirty. "Hey, sorry I'm late." He slapped his keys on the counter.

"Everything okay?" I asked.

"Sure." He grabbed his plate and headed to the microwave. "Just stuff with work, you know how it goes."

No, actually I don't.

After he ate, he hit the shower and headed for bed.

Well, that was special. Some days I feel more like a bed-and-breakfast than a wife. "Thank you patronizing April's B&B," I mumbled to myself.

Frustrated, I turned around and cleaned up the kitchen.

Friday morning, I made his coffee and lunch. I was eating breakfast when he said goodbye and announced he would be gone all weekend—again. Richard wanted help working on his basement, and some of the guys had offered to pitch in. "I felt I couldn't say no," he said and hurried out the door.

Once again, I wondered if he was being unfaithful, but I couldn't go there. *I had to keep the faith. I signed onto this marriage for better or for worse. Jesus help me to hang on. Fishing lessons, maybe that's what I'll do this weekend.*

I searched the ads until I found it again: "Fishing lessons, Saturday at 1:00 p.m. at Anderson's Lake. No experience or fishing gear required. Come learn and enjoy! Fishing licenses can be purchased on the spot."

"Sounds good," I said to Brody.

I called the number, and Lucy gave me the details and directions. I got Brody settled in and assured myself he'd be fine. I said a prayer and headed out the door.

❥

I PULLED INTO THE PARKING lot, there were several other cars there and at least a dozen people.

"Hi, I'm Mike." A man waved us over. "Everyone, please sign up here. My wife will collect your fee, and we'll get you set up with some gear."

I approached the table. "So, where do I sign up?"

"I'm Lucy," the lady responded as she extended her hand for a shake. "I'm glad you're here. We get so few women."

"Well," I said, "my husband likes to fish, so I thought this would be a nice surprise for him." I gave her my information and purchased a fishing license.

Mike talked to the class about the different types of fishing and figured out who wanted to learn what.

It turns out there's more than one way to fish. There's fly-fishing, which sounds like a lot of work, and regular fishing. I told him I just want to stand on the shore and catch fish.

Mike chuckled and said, "Yes, that is 'regular fishing.'"

I didn't realize how much went into all this fishing stuff. I opted to forego the hip waders. I did not want to go in to the lake.

After everyone signed up, they got us all set up. I could fish with live bait or lures. Apparently, different types of bait or lures attract different types of fish. This private lake was kept stocked, which made it a great place to have the class.

Lucy helped me with my pole, and then Mike took over and tried to teach me how to cast. He showed me what it looked like when he cast his line out, and I tried to do the same thing. However, when my line went zinging into the lake, it didn't make that plop sound that Mike's did. His hat was on the end of my line, so I reeled it in. He wrung out his hat, put it back on his head, and showed me again. The man had infinite patience.

On my second cast, I caught the tree above me. I was mortified.

Mike said it happens all the time.

Lucy came over and tried to show me how. *Maybe a lady can teach a lady better.*

I caught her shirt. Casting was not my strength.

Mike came over and said, "Let's try this."

He put his arms on my arms and his hands on my hands, and then it all made sense. I had the movement all wrong. That cast went zing—into the middle of the lake. I was so excited I dropped my pole and hugged him.

Lucy laughed. My fellow trainees laughed too.

I realized my mistake, grabbed my pole, and was ready for step 2. Apparently, step 2 is called *patience.* You wait and wait and wait some more. It's not a good idea to move much with live bait, so it can move on its own, if at all. Since I didn't do *still* well, I decided to try a lure.

For my first cast with the lure, I started "playing the line" like Mike and Lucy instructed me. Lo and behold, I caught a fish! Once again, I was so excited I almost dropped the pole! Almost. Lucy tried to show me how to "set the line," but I was trying to give her a one-armed hug.

We both fell into the lake.

Somehow, I came up with the pole in hand.

Lucy told me to reel in the line and start over. I tried, but it caught on something.

Mike came over and yelled, "Fish on!" He showed me how to reel it in while Lucy changed into something dry. I had never done anything like that before. It was not a huge fish, but it was fun to "fight" it. I finally understood why people liked the sport. I kept on fishing, wet jeans and all.

I caught four fish, and I got to keep them. That was enough to make a good dinner for Steve and me, so I stopped there.

Lucy returned and told me I now had to gut them, and some of them had to be scaled as well. I didn't like the gutting part, but I did get it figured out by the third one. I did the fourth one all by myself. It was a very good day.

WHEN I GOT HOME, BRODY was very happy to see me. I let him smell the catch of the day, and then I put them in the fridge in water for dinner the next night. I took a nice hot shower to wash off some of the lake and then did laundry.

"BOB357, I HAVE TO TELL you, I checked into the fishing class. It was a lot of fun. I caught four fish!"

I gave Bob a synopsis of my fishing excursion, the fun I had, the fish I caught, and the personable and helpful instructors.

"I can't thank you enough for turning me on to this. Maybe next time I go, I'll take Brody. Next, maybe I'll try camping! This outdoorsy stuff is better than I thought!"

Send.

The phone rang. Steve called to tell me he was on his way home. "Can I pick anything up?" he asked.

I was so touched. *He hasn't done that in months. Could this be a new start for us—for real?* "Would you please grab some fresh salad fixings?" I asked.

He greeted me, placed the grocery bag on the counter, and stared at the stove. "Wow, where did you get fresh fish?" he asked.

"Anderson Lake," I told him.

"Anderson's?" he asked. "That's a private lake."

"It is," I replied. "But if you pay for fishing lessons, you get to keep your catch."

"Wait, what?" He stopped washing up at the sink and looked at me. "Fishing lessons?"

"Yep, I took fishing lessons this weekend," I proudly told him. "And I caught all four of these myself. Well, mostly by myself. The first one I kind of took a lady into the lake with me."

"Okay, back up. What do you mean by you took her into the lake?"

I motioned him to the table and told him about my fishing trip.

He laughed so hard he cried. We had a wonderful meal. The whole evening, he seemed happy to be with me.

Later, as we lay in bed together, he asked, "So, what made you decide to take fishing lessons?"

"You seem to like it, and I want to be part of your world."

He got real quiet. "So, you did this for me?"

"Yes ... no ... kind of," I stuttered along. "I did it for us. I want to know what makes you tick and learn more about what you enjoy. I never understood fishing, so when a friend suggested this class, I jumped at the chance. And you know what? I really enjoyed myself. I get it now ... why you like fishing. I'm sorry I waited so long to try it. Please forgive me."

He wrapped me in his arms. "There is nothing to forgive."

How precious to my heart.

That night, the intimacy had more of that passion I had been missing.

FOR THE REST OF THE week, work kept us busy. In the mornings, Brody and I took walks. I felt like I was reinventing myself, and I really liked the new me. *I wonder what else I might like to try.*

Friday morning, Steve headed out the door, and Brody and I took off on our walk. It was a beautiful summer morning, and I wanted to make the most of it. We took a different route. It was a bit longer, sure, but I figured I had time—until we rounded the corner and came to face-to-face with a mama skunk and three babies.

I froze.

She looked me up and down and turned to Brody, and he was sizing up the situation a little differently than I was. I don't know if Brody had ever encountered a skunk before, but he took one look at Mama and decided she was a threat.

Mama apparently had the same idea about Brody. She said something to her kits, and they headed for cover. She watched them for a second, and then she turned and charged at us. It was a warning for us to back off.

Brody decided to protect me and charged at her in return.

She let us have it, full-bore. It was my first experience being skunked. *I hope it's my only experience.*

Brody turned tail and headed for home. I ran with him as Mama chased us a while. It was her way of saying, "And don't come back!"

ONCE AT THE HOUSE, I wasn't quite sure what to do. I called my mom. Brody and I waited in the front yard while she bought a bunch of tomato juice at the store and Skunk-Off at the vet's office.

She pulled into the driveway, rolled her window partway

down, and handed me the bag. "Nice-looking dog, by the way," she said. "I'd like to meet him—but not right now."

"Chicken!" I said.

"No, sweetheart, I'm a wise old woman—and don't you forget it." She rolled up her window and left.

I used my cell phone to call into work and let them know I wasn't coming in. I explained the situation to my boss. She was laughing hysterically by the time I hung up, but she let me take it off as a sick day. *How considerate.*

I kept Brody on the leash, and we headed straight to the bathroom. It was Brody's first bath in my house, and I really had no idea how it would go. Some dogs love baths. Brody, not so much. It was a fight from the beginning. I tried to lift him in, which was a comedy of errors. Or maybe the hokeypokey. I'd put foot in, and he'd take it back out. I finally got his front feet in, but when I lifted the back end, he jumped back out. We were at a standstill.

He sat on the floor, looking at me, stinking to high heaven.

With my hands on my hips, I glared back at him. Then, with my most stern pack leader voice, I said, "Listen to me, Brody MacIntyre! You will get your fuzzy butt in there right now!" I pointed to the tub. "No more arguments—I am tired of stinking." With great emphasis, I added, "Do you understand me?"

Apparently, he did. He hung his head, stepped into the tub, and sat. *Battle over!* I got in with him, still dressed, right down to my shoes. I figured my clothes weren't worth saving, and I wanted to get him scrubbed down right away.

He had taken the brunt of the spray, but after our fight getting in the tub, I figured we were even. I got Brody clean, took everything off to toss in the trash can, and scrubbed myself. Between the Skunk-Off and the tomato juice, I thought we smelled normal. I grabbed the bathroom trash and headed to the curb.

Steve pulled into the driveway and jumped out of his car. "Are you okay?" he asked, grabbing my arms. "What's going on? I called your office, and they said you were sick—and then they laughed. And what is that smell?" He talked rapidly and checked me over. "Are you okay?"

I was so touched he had rushed home, but I started laughing—and I couldn't stop.

"April, please tell me."

"Skunk." I grabbed his hand and pulled him inside.

We sat on the deck, and I brought Steve up to speed on my morning. We laughed so much Brody gave us a look halfway through and headed into the yard, either in disgust or embarrassment.

Finally, Steve got up and said, "I best head back to work. I had called you to see if you wanted to go out to dinner tonight."

"That would be nice," I said. "Do I smell okay to go public?"

"Yes, your mom saved the day." With a wink, a smile, and a peck on the lips, he was out the door.

WE WENT TO A FAMILY-STYLE restaurant.

I asked, "So, what's the special occasion?" *We haven't been out in ages.*

"You have been trying so hard lately that I thought I should too."

"Thank you, honey. That's so sweet."

He leaned in closer. "What's your plan for this weekend?"

"How about another hike on Saturday? But on Sunday morning, I'm off to church."

"Still on that church thing?" he asked.

"Yep. For now—until eternity."

"What's that supposed to mean?"

"It means I will worship God forever."

"And what happens when you die?" he asked.

I set down my glass and looked him in the eye. "Steve, what do you think happens when we die?"

He shrugged. "I don't know. They embalm you, put you in a box, bury you in the ground, and then you rot. That's pretty much it."

I shook my head. "You couldn't be further from the truth. There is a real heaven, and there is a real hell."

"You really believe that mumbo jumbo?" He plunked down his glass.

"It's true, Steve. It really is true. It's not mumbo jumbo."

"Well, *April*, I don't know about that. I think they feed you that stuff at church so you'll keep coming back and giving them money."

"There are some churches and some preachers who are in it for the money and fame, but most of them are there to teach and preach the Word of God."

"You really think so?"

"Yes. I *know* so." I stared him in the eye.

"So, you want go for a hike again tomorrow?"

"I would love that." I smiled in return.

"Are you up for more?" he challenged me.

"Why?" I asked cautiously. "What do you have in mind?"

"I know of a lake you have to hike to. The fishing's good. It's quiet. We could take Brody."

"Really? That would be perfect. Let's do it!"

That night, as I prepared for bed, I thought about our conversation. *Steve is willing to discuss Jesus with me. I think he must be searching. God must be tugging on his heart.* I asked God to give me the right words to share Him with my husband and that He would put so many Christians in his path that he would stumble over them until he fell to his knees.

5

We left on Saturday at about eight o'clock. Brody sat in the back seat of our SUV and looked quite pleased.

Steve surprised me with a pole and tackle box when he got home on Friday. So, we each carried a backpack and a fishing pole as we headed out. Brody went off leash about half a mile into the hike, but he stayed close by us.

The trail was trickier than our previous hikes; there were some steep embankments and narrow parts, but the mountain scenery was gorgeous. I pulled out my camera partway into our hike. The views were breathtaking. For the most part, we were walking a well-worn footpath, but I could tell that parts of the trail were man-made.

Once we turned the final corner, we got our first glimpse of the lake. It had a bend in it, and its shape reminded me of a boomerang. I stopped and enjoyed the view.

"They call this Elbow Lake," Steve said.

I grabbed onto him. "It's gorgeous!" I snapped off several shots.

"We still have half a mile to the lake," Steve said.

I was so energized that it didn't seem like much to me.

It was pristine. The mountain reflected on the ice-cold water. So crystal clear all the way to the bottom, the depth was hard to gauge. I had no desire to venture in. I wanted to fish from shore.

We dropped our packs at the campsite, set up a spot by the fire pit, and then set up to fish. I had explained my reasons for lure fishing over live bait, and my new tackle box contained some good lures for the fish that were supposed to be in this lake. We spaced ourselves out and started fishing.

I felt so close to God in this quiet, peaceful, and serene place. I knew He was right there with me. It was like no place I had ever been. I *knew* God was there. *How could anyone look around at that beautiful creation and* not *feel God's presence?*

"What's got you smiling like that?" Steve asked.

"Can't you feel it?"

"Feel what?"

"God."

"God?" he retorted.

"God's presence, right here?" I gestured to the magnificent scenery.

"We're out in nature; it's Mother Nature," he replied.

"Oh, please, that's a cop-out." I sounded more disgusted than I intended. "That's what people say when they want to give credit to a Creator but don't want to acknowledge God for what He is."

"Oh really?" His voice dripped with sarcasm.

"Yes, really," I said calmly. "Romans says creation speaks of Him, so we are without excuse. God is in His creation all the time. We can never say we never saw God."

Right at that moment, an eagle flew over the lake. I followed its flight. It was another gift from God, and I knew it.

"I don't know, April. Pretty hard for me to swallow. I've always been told a man takes care of himself."

"He won't force Himself on you. He'll wait for you to let Him in." Right at that moment, I got a strike. "Fish on!"

WE FISHED UNTIL WE HAD both caught our limit for the day. Afterward, we gathered some branches and other firewood from the forest floor. Steve got a fire going and grilled our catch. We set out Brody's dish of dog food while we ate our fish. We chatted, relaxed, and drank in the beauty around us. Brody got treats before we headed back down.

What a wonderful day. Thank you, Jesus.

SUNDAY MORNING, AS I STARTED getting ready for church, Steve leaned against the bathroom doorjamb.

"You're welcome to go with me," I said.

He shook his head. "I've got things to do."

Once again, I went my way, and he went his.

When I got home, he wasn't there. He returned around three thirty, but I didn't ask where he'd been—and he didn't offer. I prayed it wasn't another woman.

As the week wore on, I wondered about the weekend. Every other weekend, he left me for an overnight, which worried me.

On Thursday night, I gathered up my courage and asked, "What are you doing this weekend?"

"I'll be out of town," he said.

I asked him, "More stuff with Richard?"

"No, Richard's nephew, Noah," he replied. "He works with us. He's got the bumper sticker I told you about. He needs some help remodeling his cabin. His wife's expecting soon, and he wants to get it all done before the baby comes. Some of us guys said we'd pitch in to help."

A plausible explanation, but I didn't know what to believe.

Sure enough, on Friday night, right after dinner, he was out the door. He said he had to get there so they could start bright and early in the morning. I had a bad feeling. Am I jumping to conclusions? Perhaps he is telling me the truth. Or he has a girlfriend and is using these "good deeds" as cover stories. *Oh God, please help me. Tell me what to do.*

SATURDAY MORNING, I PLANNED TO go to the hardware store about the leaky faucet and the back door. Tackling another something new, this "April reinvented" thing took on a new level. I went online to learn a little about the lingo, so I didn't walk in saying, "The thingamabob is dripping, and my door doesn't work right." Women get enough grief for not knowing how to fix things. But first, I decided to sign off on the dating site.

"A251, I'm glad you tried fishing. I'd love to see a video of that day. I laughed as I read your email. Good for you trying more outdoor stuff. A chance for adventure and getting close to God."

"Bob357, it's so funny you should mention that. I went for another hike and more fishing this past weekend. I felt so close to God. This weekend, I am tackling plumbing and carpentry. Wish me luck. I'm off to the hardware store now."

Send.

AT THE HARDWARE STORE, I walked into the section that looked like plumbing parts.

"Hello, ma'am. Can I help you?" a welcome voice said.

I saw a name tag. "Kendra, I'm April. To start with, I've got a leaky faucet."

Kendra knew her stuff.

Soon, I headed for my car with a small bag in hand: a new washer for my faucet and longer screws to hold the door in place. I suspected a bit of wood rot, and Kendra and the internet agreed with me. As I headed home, my confidence was in high gear. *How uplifting to talk to another woman. I can really do this.*

OKAY, FAUCET FIRST. I THINK I found all the right tools in Steve's toolbox. Wow, getting this thing to budge is a lot harder than I thought, but with determination, I kept working.

Faucet's done! Yeah! And look: no drips! Yee-haw!

"Hey, Brody, would you look at that? Your mom can fix something—all by herself. A regular handywoman."

He lifted his head off his paws, tilted it to one side, and then returned to his original position of rest. *Obviously not impressed.*

"Onto the door," I said. No response.

I don't think Brody understood we were having a conversation, but I kept talking. "Now, how does this screw gun thing work?" I hit a button, and it made a whirring sound when I hit the trigger. "Got it!" I backed out the first screw and held it out to Brody. "Holy cow! Would you look at how small that screw is. No wonder it wasn't working right. The door's too heavy for these little screws to hold it together right. But there *is* some wood rot, so I'll talk to Steve about replacing jambs someday soon."

Brody flopped on his side with a big heave.

"Hey, Brody, check it out. I'm using power tools."

Brody remained sleeping on the floor. Not even a twitch in response.

"Tough crowd," I muttered.

BRODY RESTED IN THE SUN as I lounged on the deck, read my Bible, and sipped a cup of tea. I have to say I was surprised by my easy fixes. It was a boost to my confidence to do a job I had been asking Steve to do for six months. *I spent more time asking him than I did doing it!*

Then, I was struck by a thought. I hoped God wasn't preparing me to be alone. I still loved my husband, and I wanted my marriage to work. We were two weeks away from our anniversary. I had to wonder if he would be gone that weekend too. *Would he spend our anniversary with another woman?*

My goodness, listen to me. I have no proof, only speculation. I had all but named this woman and imagined all kinds of things, like these alternate weekends happening when her kids were with their dad.

Snap out of it, April!

I stood up, grabbed my phone, and dialed.

"Hey, Mom? Listen, Brody and I were going to go for a walk. I can stop by your place first so you can meet him. He doesn't smell anymore—thanks to you and your bag of miracles."

"I would love to see you both, dear," she replied.

I hung up the phone and called Brody in from the backyard.

He came running.

When we pulled up at my mom's house, she was working on her flower garden.

Brody jumped out of the car and headed right for her. They seemed to hit it off right away.

"Mom, this is Brody, your grand-puppy."

"Well, at least I got a grand-something!" She rubbed his head and ears.

"I know, Mom. Maybe June and her husband will give you grandbabies, but I don't think you'll be getting any from my house anytime soon. So, enjoy this guy."

"He is a beautiful dog. How old is he?" she asked.

"The shelter didn't know for sure. Their best guess was four or five. A lot of rescue dogs don't come with clear records."

"He's a sweetheart, and he doesn't smell anymore."

"No, he doesn't. Thank you so much for helping us out the other day," I replied.

"I've thought about getting a dog again," Mom said as we headed inside. "My house seems so quiet, and the company would be nice too."

"It's been five years, Mom. You should get a dog—or a boyfriend!" I grinned.

"No thanks on the boyfriend, but this guy makes me want another dog." She rubbed Brody's side, and he leaned into her. "I forgot how lovable they are."

"Yeah, like God's love for us: total and unconditional."

"That's true. Would you go to the shelter with me?"

"Of course. I would love that. Just let me know when."

"Where are you guys off to today?" She leaned over and brushed dirt and grass from her knees.

"To the park. He loves it. And I want to see if he'll fetch a ball or a Frisbee. I keep trying new things with him to see how he reacts in different situations."

"What's Steve up to today?"

"He's helping a friend remodel his cabin."

"He's a good carpenter. Good of him to share his talent."

"Yep, good for him," I replied curtly. "Well, Brody and I are going to take off. See you later, Mom."

With a hug and a kiss, we headed to the park. I was hoping we could both get some exercise. Skunk-free exercise, that is.

The park was busy. Lots of other people were there with family and furry family. I tried the Frisbee, but he didn't quite get the idea. The tennis ball was another story. He played fetch until my arm was tired and his tongue was hanging out.

WHEN STEVE RETURNED HOME ON Sunday, he looked as tired as Brody had been the day before. *Dog-tired.* I felt for the guy. I was just setting the table for dinner. Steve filled his plate with spaghetti and grabbed a glass of milk. I followed suit. We sat at the table. I bowed my head in prayer. I was shocked when Steve bowed his head too.

"How did the remodeling go?" I asked.

"Fine, we got a lot done."

"When is his wife due?"

"In a few weeks. I don't remember exactly, but soon."

He didn't seem interested in conversation, so I gave up. We finished our meal in silence. He cleared his place and headed for the shower. When he returned to the living room, he flopped in his chair and fell asleep for about an hour. When he woke up, he headed for bed.

6

Tuesday night, we were at the dinner table. I said, "Steve, I got the faucet and the door fixed this weekend."

He looked at me in shock, "Excuse me? You did what?"

I said, "The faucet had a bad washer, and the screws in the doorjamb were way too small. I replaced them. It works fine now, although I think there's some wood rot at the bottom."

He stood up and started pacing. "When did you get so handy?"

I tried to stay calm. I had obviously hit a nerve, and I didn't know how or why. "Well, I wanted it done, and you seemed too busy. I checked online and bought the supplies at the hardware store. The lady I dealt with there was really great, and she got me all lined out."

"Wow, really? You just trotted yourself down to the hardware store and 'got everything all lined out'?" He turned again, still pacing.

"I'm sorry, are you mad about this?"

"Mad?" The volume rose in his voice. "Why would I be mad? My wife finds ways to replace me every time I turn around. Pretty soon, you won't even miss me or want me to come home."

I stood up and placed my hand on his arm. "Steve, I don't

know where this is coming from, but that's not true. I love you, and I want you here. I want you in my life. You own a piece of my heart."

"Oh great, and who owns the other piece? The guy at the hardware store?" He stormed out of the room.

I really didn't understand what had happened. *I mean, really, what am I supposed to do while he's out and about? Sit around and moan and groan that he's not here? Life doesn't wait when you're not looking. You either join in or get run over. I refuse to be a hit-and-run case on the streets of life. I want to be an active participant in mine. I wish my husband did too.*

I DIDN'T MENTION ANYTHING ABOUT the repairs again, but Wednesday morning, I caught him checking out the back door.

"You did a good job, April. I'm sorry I didn't do it for you. And I'm sorry I was a heel last night."

"Yeah." I leaned my hip against the kitchen counter and crossed my arms. "You were a real heel, and you really hurt my feelings. I don't know what I did that upset you, but I didn't mean to. I got tired of waiting for you to have the time. I'm not going to nag you to do something I can do myself."

"But that's my point. You keep learning to do stuff for yourself, and pretty soon, you won't need me anymore." He thumped his chest.

I put my arms around him and said, "I'm not married to you so you can fix things for me. I'm here, with you, because I love you and want to share my life with you."

He grabbed me and wrapped me in a big hug. "I don't deserve you, April." It felt good to be in his arms.

I smiled up at him, "Yeah, you probably do."

He hugged me tighter.

AT DINNER THURSDAY NIGHT, STEVE suggested another hike on Saturday.

I eagerly said yes.

Brody, who seemed to understand the word *hike*, let out a bark. He plodded over to Steve, leaned against his legs, looked up at him, and wagged his tail. It was an obvious plea to be included.

Steve and I locked eyes and laughed.

"Yes, Brody, you can come too." He petted him and rubbed his side.

SATURDAY WAS GORGEOUS. WE WENT to a different lake to fish, hiked to a campsite, and cooked our lunch. A nice, quiet spot. No distractions from the world.

"So, what do you want do for our anniversary next weekend?" I asked.

I thought I detected a pained looked on his face, but he shook it off quickly.

"What would you like to do? Seven years, right?"

"Yeah, that scary number seven." I decided it was time to dive into the deep end. "I was wondering if you wanted to try camping and fishing. Do we have all the gear we need?"

"Really?" A sincere shock in his voice. "You want to go camping?"

"I used to enjoy it as a kid, and I like to fish now, so I think it's time to try. What do you think?"

I could see the wheels turning in his head as he counted our inventory on his fingers. "We have a tent, three sleeping bags, fishing poles, and coolers, so I think we'd be set. We just need to grab some grub."

Excited that he was willing to go along with my suggestion so readily, I asked, "What kind of grub? What can we cook out there besides fish? Hot dogs? Steaks? Burgers? You tell me. I'm the newbie here."

"Okay, here's what we can do." He leaned closer to me, getting into the spirit of the adventure. "We'll need eggs, potatoes, and bread for breakfasts. Maybe some of that instant pancake mix. You decide. Then get steaks and hot dogs, and that should cover it. Can you make a couple of salads?"

"Potato salad or green salad?"

"Can you do one of each?" he asked. "We could have a real nice dinner for our anniversary and something more casual the next night."

"We are talking two nights in the woods?" I was worried about being away from my bed and my shower for that long.

"Yep, are you up for it?"

"How hard is the ground going to be?"

"Take an extra blanket or two—and you'll be fine."

He sounded so sure, and I wanted to believe him.

THE FISHING WAS GOOD, AND our anniversary dinner was awesome.

Steve set up a grate over part of the fire and grilled our steaks on it.

I had researched a way to bake potatoes in the fire. I cut them in half, added butter, onions, and seasoning, and wrapped the whole mess in tinfoil. They cooked on a bank of coals like a regular baked potato. We added our green salad and yum, yum! *What a treat!*

Afterward, we sat around the fire pit, relaxing, while Brody gnawed on a bone. We could hear crickets, frogs, and owls. I don't know if it was the fresh air or what, but before I knew it, I was about to doze off, right there. "I'm heading for bed before I fall asleep in the fire."

Steve replied, "I'll douse the fire and be right in."

I pulled back the tent flap, settled into my sleeping bag, and reminded myself that Steve said sleeping like this would be fine.

Now, let's just be clear. There are different definitions of "fine." Hard ground with roots and rocks was not my definition of fine. Also, I didn't realize that when outdoors, you are the only one trying to sleep. The owls are hunting, the coyotes are talking trash, and I'm pretty sure I heard a wolf howl and a cougar, which sounded like a person screaming. It all seemed rather innocuous in the daytime, but at night, this paradise comes alive. I felt like an item on a buffet menu. Meanwhile, Brody paced and whined in the tent. The so-called six-man tent with two adults and a pacing dog made it feel like a shoebox. So, the whole "sleep comfortably" idea was a crock!

The animals quieted down at about two that morning, but it started to rain. The soft drizzle on the tent cover was so peaceful and soothing. I was lulled into a deep sleep in short order. Brody was too.

I MUST SAY, WAKING UP in the mountains after a light rain is an incredible experience. Sure, every muscle hurt from sleeping on the ground, but the air smelled heavenly, the birds were singing, and the sky was cloudy but gorgeous.

Steve sat by the fire, a pot of coffee cooking, when I crawled out of the tent. I stretched and smiled. "I'm so glad I didn't miss this."

He smiled at me as he handed me a cup of fresh coffee. "I figured you were ready to pack it in about midnight."

I hugged the coffee cup with my hands. "I was pretty close. Brody was making a bad situation worse."

"It's probably his first camping trip. He'll get better at it." Steve gave Brody a good-morning hug.

"I hope so." I rubbed my back.

"Does that mean you're willing to do this again?" Steve asked.

I raised up one hand and waved it in the air. "No, I don't want to do *this* again. I wouldn't mind camping again, but this whole tree-roots-in-the-back routine is not going to cut it. There's got to be a comfortable way!"

"Well, they do have mats—and air mattresses."

"Wait, what?" Was he holding out on me? "How would you get an air mattress up here?"

"You bring it up in your pack and inflate it on-site. You can get one with a pump."

"Hmmm. Sounds worthy of research." I took another sip of my coffee.

Steve laughed. "Internet beware! April's on the hunt!"

After breakfast, we took a short hike to loosen up our sore muscles and fished for our lunch. We packed it up after dinner since I did not want to sleep on that hard ground again—and I didn't want to miss church.

We got back to the house and unloaded. Steve took off to "run some really quick errands." He was gone for a couple hours, got home, and hit the showers.

I was already in bed, exhausted. Sleep came quick for both of us.

SUNDAY MORNING, I MADE OMELETS, toast, and coffee. We sat down at the table, and he asked, "Church again?"

"Yes, sir. Want to come along?"

"What do you do there?" he asked.

I tried to hide my surprise. "We visit. We go to classes. After Sunday school, everyone heads into the sanctuary. We sing. The preacher gives his sermon, we sing a closing hymn, and we go home. It's really rather painless."

"Aren't you a little old for Sunday school?" He cocked his eyebrow.

"It's for all ages." I reached for my coffee cup. "We're all still learning. What else would you call it?"

He put jam on his toast and said, "I don't know … adult school?"

I laughed. "Oh yeah, that sounds so much better."

He laughed too. "Okay, it does sound silly. But Sunday school sounds like something kids go to."

"Well, we are all God's children, so I guess it's okay."

"See, that's the kind of stuff I don't like." His words had a harsh edge. "All church people say stuff like that. It's like they're talking in code, and the rest of us stand around looking at them like we don't know the secret."

I put my hand on top of his. "Oh, Steve, I'd love to tell you the secret. The love of Jesus is an awesome thing, but it's not a secret. It's been put down in writing for all to see. You just have to want it."

"I know. He's knocking on the door of my head," he said.

I smiled. "Well, I've heard of knocking on the door of your heart, but head works too … because you have to take it into your head first and then let it into your heart."

"Well, have a good time." He was up and out the door.

I'm not sure if I am making headway with him or pushing him away. But the Bible tells me if a believer is married to a nonbeliever and the nonbeliever wishes to stay in the marriage, you've got to keep hanging on. That's the paraphrased "April version." I may not always be able to tell you chapter and verse, but I can usually find it in my Bible. I know the Word and have it in my heart and my head, which sure makes tough situations easier to handle. Sweet Jesus, help me to have the words to help my husband. Amen.

7

After church, Steve still wasn't home, so I went online to check out air mattresses—and to finally get off the dating site. *I am really going to do it this time.* I found air mattresses at a store in town and printed out the information. Then I went to my communications with Bob357.

"A251, hello! Wow, it seems like you aren't on here very often. Good to hear from you. I guess that's a good sign, right? We're getting to know each other nice and slow. How's the dog doing?"

"Hello, Bob357. Brody's good. He sleeps and earns his treats. You just got to love 'em and spoil 'em, right? How are things with you?"

What? Why did I ask him that? I came on here to sign off this place! I can't keep doing this. This is wrong. It's like I'm cheating. But Bob357 and I have never talked about meeting up in real life. We just chat. He's just a friend. And to be honest, I've needed that friend.

"Oh, and guess what, I went camping, the whole 'one with nature' thing. It's not all it's cracked up to be. The ground was horribly hard and uncomfortable. I got up the next morning hurting in places I didn't even know I could hurt! If, and when, I do that again, it will include an air mattress."

Send.

I just can't delete my contact with Bob357 yet. He seems like such a nice guy, and if it weren't for him, I wouldn't have Brody or have learned to fish. Both of those things have brought me closer to Steve. Speaking of Steve, I wonder where he is.

Steve got home just before dinner. I told him about the air mattresses at the sporting goods store and handed him the printout.

He said, "I'll check it out tomorrow after work."

Good, he is taking an interest.

Monday, Steve came home late—with a large bag from Outdoor Gear and a large smile.

"Queen-sized one, baby. I almost got two twin-sized mattresses, but I thought it would be easier to blow up one. Check it out."

"Sure thing, but after dinner."

After we ate, Steve helped me with the dishes.

"What brought this on?" I couldn't help but ask.

"I want us to hurry and check out the air mattress." His excitement touched me as we headed to the living room.

We took everything out of the box, pushed the couch and chairs out of the way, and blew up the mattress. The pump was easy to operate. We could do it out in the woods with no power. Next thing I knew, we had blankets and pillows and were lying in the living room on our new air mattress, watching a movie, and snuggling. My heart was singing. Here we were, like a couple of kids, all excited about a new toy. We had a lovely intimate encounter and slept right there that night.

The rest of the week, we planned our next campout. Steve was there with me—totally. I didn't think, not even once, about whether or not there was another woman. *No way he could be that attentive and loving and be cheating on me.*

We packed everything, except the cooler, on Thursday

night. We planned to leave right after work on Friday. I was doing just that on Friday when the phone rang. I answered it, but no one said anything, so I hung up. That happened twice more before Steve got home. I was getting Brody's things together when the phone rang again.

"I think it's one of those telemarketers. They keep calling, but no one says anything."

Steve answered the phone and apparently got a response. He took the phone into the garage to talk. By the time I got the SUV all packed up, he was hanging up. He looked kind of stressed out.

"Things okay at work, hon?"

"Yeah. Just business stuff, you know how it is."

"Is our camping trip still on?" I asked.

"Absolutely. Let's go."

He shook it off, and away we went.

"Where are we going?" I asked.

He grabbed my hand and smiled. "I thought we'd camp by the river. The guys at work told me about a nice place. The fishing is supposed to be good, and there's some nice camping spots."

I was all for it.

We pulled off the main road and went several miles down a dirt road. We parked, grabbed our gear, and hiked another half a mile. We found a nice, wide, flat spot to set up camp with a fire pit nearby. It was right by the river. Before long, we had enough fish for supper, and we decided to hike around.

Brody chased after a few rabbits and squirrels, but we made too much noise to see any big game.

As we were cooking our dinner over the fire, Steve asked, "April, have you ever thought about having kids?"

I was kind of shocked. We hadn't discussed kids in ages.

"Sure, someday. Why?"

"No reason." He shrugged.

"I would love to have a little mini-me and mini-you running around some day. That was part of the plan, right?"

"Yeah, I guess so." He seemed to be working something out in his mind. "We've been so busy. But now, with Brody, I see the responsibility, the care, and the joy you get in return … I guess it wouldn't be that scary to have kids."

I was surprised by his confession. "Is that why you wanted to wait? Because it scared you?"

"Well, yeah, it is scary." He couldn't quite make eye contact. "All this responsibility, and what if we mess it up? Or what if something happens to us? I would hate to put our kids through what my folks put me and my sister through."

"Not all marriages end up in divorce, Steve."

"No, only about 50 percent. Not every marriage is like what your folks had: forty years of true love. That's an incredible thing. I'm sure they'd still be sweethearts … if it hadn't been for the cancer."

"Agreed. Not everyone meets the love of their life in junior high. I worry about my mom though. She's still young … not even sixty-five yet. She could find someone new to love, but she doesn't even want to think about it. Though she did ask me to go with her to the shelter to pick out a dog."

"A dog would be good company. I worry about her."

"Me too."

The subject of kids didn't come up again.

After dinner, we headed to the tent. The air mattress made the space inside seem smaller, but it was worth it. Brody had his own sleeping bag on the floor. The soothing sound of the river quickly lulled us into a peaceful sleep.

At daylight, I rolled over and reached for Steve. He was

already out of bed. When I came out of the tent, he was brewing coffee by the fire.

"Good morning, sunshine." He offered me a steaming mug. *I can't think of any better way to start a day than listening to water rush by, enjoying the fresh air and wilderness, and sipping a fresh cup of coffee.* "This is so perfect. So serene. I'm sorry we waited so long to do this kind of stuff."

"I didn't know you liked this kind of stuff—or we would have."

"Well, I didn't know either, but I do. I like this. Speaking of things you don't know about me, I also love to watch football. My favorite team is the Raiders. I hope they can finally get a good coach-quarterback scenario and get back to winning games."

"You like football? Since when?"

I shrugged. "Oh, I don't know. You kept talking about it and going to games with your friends, so I started watching. I don't understand all of it, but I'd be glad to learn."

"Wow, really! Why the Raiders?"

"They have the classiest uniforms. And they play good."

"You do know they haven't had a winning season in a while, right?"

"I know, but I see their potential."

"Okay, fair enough. What else should I know about you? Are you a trophy hunter too?" He winked.

"No, I don't hunt. I don't like guns and don't want to kill anything. I do my hunting at the grocery store. It's a lot less work. That's also where I do my gardening. They do a wonderful job of weeding and watering."

Steve grinned. "That's the girl I fell in love with: smart, a quirky sense of humor, and easy on the eyes."

After our breakfast of bacon and eggs, we cleaned up

camp and did some fishing. We both caught our limit, packed everything up, and took off for a short hike. We discovered a nice spot full of blackberries. Steve returned to camp for a container. We picked about half a gallon, and then we headed home.

8

I called Mom Monday morning before I left for work and asked her to join me for lunch.

"Yes, dear. I would love that," she replied, "When and where?"

"Oh, let's say eleven-thirty at the café on Sixth Street," I suggested. "That way, we'll beat the lunch crowd."

"That sounds good. I'll see you there."

I told the office I was taking a longer lunch, and when I pulled into the parking lot, Mom was reading a book in her car. I knocked on her window.

She jumped, screamed, and threw her book to the other side of the car. She rolled down the window. "April! You scared me half to death!"

"Sorry, Mom." I laughed.

We went into the restaurant and were seated. I ordered a burger, fries, and soda while she had a chicken salad and tea. *I know I need to learn to eat healthier, but not at this moment.*

"Okay, April, what's going on?" she said. "It's been forever since you invited me to lunch. Is everything okay?"

I tried to sound nonchalant. "Yes, Mom. What could be wrong?"

"Well, let's see. Your house has termites, your dog has fleas, your husband is having an affair, you're losing your job, your house, your teeth." She was getting more revved up. "You could be pregnant. Is that it? Are you pregnant? Oh, April!"

I threw my hands up, trying to stop her tirade. "Mom, hold the phone. That's not it. None of it. Calm down a little, okay?"

"Okay." She primped and put her napkin on her lap, looking like a lady at a tea. "I'm calm. What's up?"

"I just wanted to talk to you a little bit about marriage. You and Dad were married forever. Did you guys ever have struggles?"

"Oh honey," she placed her hand on mine, "every marriage has struggles. Nothing grows without growing pains. That includes marriage. Matter of fact, when you were about a year old, your dad and I were having such a hard time of it that we almost got divorced."

"What? I've never heard this before."

She looked pensive. "It's not the type of thing a person usually shares with their children, but I will share my story if you promise not to judge me."

"Of course, Mom. I would never do that."

"Okay, here goes." She heaved a big sigh. "June was about three, and you were a year old. Your dad didn't know Jesus yet. I was going to church, and there was a nice young couple there. Her name was Mary, and she was a sweetheart. His name was Ron, and boy, was he a looker. He had the bluest eyes and the cutest dimples." She had a starstruck look for a second and then shook it off. "They had two kids about the same age as you and June. Ron would always take the kids to the nursery or pick them up. He treated Mary like she was a treasure to him. I couldn't even get your father to talk about church with me, much less attend. I was so jealous that I developed a crush on Ron—"

"So what, Mom?" I interrupted. "What woman hasn't had a crush now and again?"

"Just listen. I was falling out of love with your dad and seriously falling for this guy. I thought about him. I dreamed about him. I even drove by where he worked so I could see him. I saw him walk into a restaurant one day and followed him in, hoping I could talk to him."

"You were stalking him?" I asked.

"I guess that is what they call it now, but I was obsessed. I didn't want to end his marriage, or mine, but I wanted what Ron and Mary had. Then, one day, at lady's Bible study, Mary was real quiet like. I asked her what was wrong. She started pouring her heart out to me, telling me Ron was a workaholic. Mary and the kids only got to see him on the weekends. The rest of the week, he was gone from six in the morning to eight at night. She said it was really wearing on her and on their relationship. That's when I realized no marriage is perfect. Just because he seemed perfect at church, the reality was quite different. I went home, and I told your dad about my emotional affair. At first, he laughed at me. Ron didn't even know I existed. I think he said hi to me once, but that was it. But Jesus said if we lust in our hearts, it's the same thing as adultery. And I had done just that.

"I cried and cried and asked your father's forgiveness. He finally took me in his arms and apologized for not being a better husband. We started making some changes—small ones—but each little thing made a difference. About two years later, he went to church with me. It was the beginning of your father accepting Christ. You were five when he was baptized. I know you don't remember those early years, but some of them were hard. Yes, we were high school sweethearts, but that doesn't mean it was all sunshine and roses. There were a lot of thorns among those roses, dear."

"But I don't ever remember seeing you and Dad fight. It always seemed like things were perfect between you guys."

"Oh, honey, we had our share of spats. Neither of us were prone to yelling, but that doesn't mean there weren't some tough times. When Grandpa Jim came to live with us during the last years of his life, there was a lot of stress. It required a lot more out of us than we first realized, but we were so grateful we got to have that time with him. Life is full of challenges. Every marriage is going to have hard times. It's part of the growth of love. You've got to have rain to see a rainbow."

I hesitated to speak my true thoughts, "It's just that … Steve seems so preoccupied with things outside our home that he doesn't want to be inside our home … with me."

"So, what are you doing about it?" she challenged.

"Excuse me?" That wasn't the sympathy I thought I was going to get.

"Well, did you expect me to say, 'Oh, baby, I'm so sorry? Stick it out'? I'm not going to give that advice to anyone. If you are struggling in your marriage, you need to decide." She started counting on her fingers. "One, do I want to be here? Two, do I want my marriage to work? Three, what am I willing to do to make it work? If you sit by passively and hope, somehow, things will magically be fixed, you'll end up sad and alone.

"Start with prayer, but remember God always uses people to make things happen. He could have created new people after the flood, but He chose Noah and his family to repopulate the earth. He chose Moses and Aaron to lead His people out of Egypt, and He chose Joseph and Mary to raise Jesus. What makes you think He wouldn't use you to reach your husband?

God calls us to be active participants in our lives—so be active. Do something."

"Well, I have kind of already started that process. I took fishing lessons, and Steve and I have gone fishing a couple times. We even went camping. It was great. I felt like we were reconnecting again. And I got to share about God with him on a few occasions. He wasn't totally resistant. It's a start. But please be praying for Steve and me."

"Oh, sweetheart." She looked at me with her Mom smile. "I already do that every day. God will work this out. I don't know what all the struggles are, and I don't have to know, but God already knows—and He is there for you. Let the Holy Spirit guide you. Trust Him."

"I do, Mom. I do. I just wish Steve knew Jesus too."

"Once your dad came to Jesus, things were better, but they still weren't perfect. Remember, marriage is a couple of sinners trying to figure it out together. That's the key: *together.*"

"Oh, Mom, thank you."

"You need a weekend away with a girlfriend," she responded.

"Oh no. I don't have any girlfriends. Not anymore."

"I never have understood that. You and Chloe were inseparable in high school, and then in college, it was all over."

"Catching her in our dorm room with my boyfriend kind of ruined the friendship."

"I know. But why didn't you ever develop another friendship? You two were inseparable. I think you would miss that."

"I don't know. It was just hard to completely trust another girlfriend after the whole Chloe and Cliff scenario."

"Speaking of Cliff, I saw his mom the other day. He and Chloe are getting a divorce. She left him for another man."

"Well, I'm sorry for him and his kids, but I'm not surprised. She cheated *with* him. It's only logical she would cheat *on* him."

"That sounds bitter."

"You know what they say, 'Once a cheater, always a cheater.'"

"Chloe turned out to be not such a good friend. The Chloe I grew up with and the college Chloe were different. The whole thing with Cliff was the last straw. And I do have girlfriends, Mom. It's just different. Well, I better go. Thank you for lunch—and for the talk. I really needed this. I love you."

We walked out to our cars together, hugged again, and said our goodbyes.

On my way back to work, I kept thinking about what my mom had said. *I need to be active in making our marriage better. I think I've had a good start on that. If I am right about the whole affair thing, Steve will have another excuse to be gone this weekend. And I really need to get off that dating site. Mom is right. Cheating in your mind is still cheating. Just because I haven't met this man doesn't make it any less lethal.*

If Steve finds out I was on a dating site, he would be crushed. I know I would be if I found out he was doing the same thing. And I owe the truth to Bob357. I have used him, and it's unfair to him. He's a nice man, and he deserves better than a lonely, married woman.

9

Steve hadn't made any comments about the weekend yet, but by Thursday, I couldn't wait any longer.

He came through the door, right on time. "Hey, babe. Dinner smells good. What's on the menu?"

I recited, "Chicken-fried chicken, potatoes, gravy, and corn on the cob."

He rubbed his belly. "Sounds delicious."

At the table, we talked about our day and the work challenges we faced.

"So," I started, "plans for this weekend?"

"Yeah. Noah and his brothers have a traditional guys' weekend. And, with Noah's wife being pregnant, he might not get another chance soon. It should be fun. I'll leave right after dinner tomorrow night."

"Oh, okay." I was crushed, sure that my fears were confirmed, "Well, I hope that's a good time for you. What are you doing?"

"We're going up to his cabin, the one we worked on. It's a couple hours north of here on the lake."

"Well, maybe we could go there sometime together."

"Yeah, we'll see."

We ended our meal in silence. I couldn't help but wonder again. *Is this an affair? Am I making more of this than there is?*

Steve has been so wonderful with me since Brody came into our lives. It can't be true. Dear Lord, please save my marriage.

Friday morning, as Steve left for work, he gave me a kiss and said goodbye. It all seemed so normal. I hoped and prayed I was wrong about the affair.

When I got home from work that evening, I knew it was time to go online and level with Bob357.

"A251, good to hear from you. You're on here so rarely that I was wondering if you found yourself another man already! Did you find an air mattress? Do you want to try camping again? Maybe with a friend this time?"

Okay, time to level with him. Bite the bullet, April.

"Bob357, I feel like such a heel. I'm only on here today to tell you that I won't be coming back on again. I haven't been honest with you, and for that I feel like the lowest form of scum. I am asking for your forgiveness. When I signed up on this site, it was as kind of a dare. My husband and I were watching one of their commercials, and he said, 'I wonder if they would match us up.' I thought that meant he wanted me to sign up and find him on here. But, as time went by, I wondered if he wanted me to sign up and find someone else because I think he's having an affair. I don't have any actual proof, but I have a lot of circumstantial evidence.

"But I have to thank you. Because of you, I have Brody— and I learned to fish. That has brought my husband and me closer together. Not close enough, though, because I think he's with 'her' right now. But I am going to fight for my marriage, and I can't do that if I'm distracted by you. You are the only friend I made on this site, and I am so grateful for you. Please forgive me for using you this way, but I'm not sorry we became friends. Maybe someday we can meet in real life, and then you can meet my husband and my dog. And, if it's not too much, can I ask a favor? Would you please pray for us? Steve and I have been married seven years, and I hope this is just a seven-year itch he had to scratch. I will be praying the Lord leads the right woman to you."

Send.

I signed off and deleted my account without waiting for a reply. *It doesn't matter anyway. I can't let myself be distracted by someone else. If I'm sharing my hopes and dreams with someone other than my husband, I am being unfaithful to him—and I refuse to let that continue. Goodbye Bob357, I will miss you. God, help me know what to do. Help me, Lord, be the wife my husband needs. My fervent hope and prayer Lord is that he comes to know You as his Savior. Please help us, Lord. Amen.*

I had a whole weekend to myself and wondered what to do. I snapped my fingers and jumped. I picked up the phone and dialed. "Mom, what are you doing tomorrow?"

"What do you have in mind?" she asked.

I jumped right in. "It's time we got you a dog. I'll pick you up around nine, and we'll head to the shelter."

"Sounds good to me."

SATURDAY, BRODY AND I TOOK a nice skunk-free walk. After breakfast and a shower, I headed over to Mom's.

She was all ready and raring to go.

"I talked to June about this last night." She seemed almost giddy. "She is happy for me. It seems kind of silly, but I'm excited."

"It's not silly. You are going to meet a new companion … and … make a difference in some dog's life forever. Pretty cool stuff. I know I'm so glad we got Brody. I forgot how much I missed having a dog."

"Do you think they know?" she asked as we headed to the car.

"I don't know. They may think those cages will be all there is for them, but I can tell you this: Brody is so grateful and so loving every day. He brings us a lot of joy."

"Okay," she said, buckling up. "Let's do this."

It took us about half an hour to get to the shelter. The gate was open. We heard even more barking than when I was there last time. *How can they could fit so many dogs in there?* The same lady who helped me with Brody rushed up to us. "Hi, ladies. Thank God you're here."

"What's going on?" Mom asked.

"We confiscated animals from two puppy mills in one week," she explained. "We normally house between twenty-five and thirty dogs, but we have fifty-two right now!"

We walked towards the building. "What is a puppy mill?" I asked.

"People get purebred dogs and keep them in deplorable conditions. They breed the females to have litter after litter, some starting as young as a year old. It's not healthy for the moms or the babies, and there is often a lot of inbreeding, which creates medical problems too. We have to bathe and inspect each dog." She ran her hand through her hair. "We have a lot of work to do today."

"Excuse me, ma'am," my mom said, "are you expecting us to work today?"

"Isn't that why you're here?"

"No ... but what can we do?"

"Oh, are you here to adopt?"

"I am. My daughter already has a dog."

"Oh, yes. That's why you looked familiar."

"A shepherd mix named Brody," I replied.

"I remember Brody—a real sweetheart. Look, we really do need the help. You can take some extra time with the dogs so you get to know them better before you choose."

Spoken like a good saleswoman.

My mom jumped in. "Lead the way. I'm Joyce, and this is my daughter, April."

"I'm Cindy, and I can't thank you enough. They told me they were sending volunteers first thing this morning. I assumed you were some of them."

I smiled. "Well, Cindy, now we are."

Cindy showed us around. Each dog needed to be bathed and have its toenails trimmed. Some needed haircuts. More volunteers showed up right after we did, and stations were set up. Some vets volunteered for exams. One station provided shots. Another one checked for leash training and assessing temperament. Mom and I spent most of the day there.

At lunchtime, everyone chipped in a few bucks, and we had pizzas and drinks delivered. Mom and I enjoyed our visits with the other volunteers, who were all dog lovers like us. Some were professional dog groomers and trainers.

About three o'clock, Mom tapped me on the shoulder. I looked up from the dog I was bathing.

"I'm going to foster some of these puppies," she announced. "Two females with young litters. I'm going to take them home with me."

"And what are they going to do when you're at work?" I asked.

"I talked to Cindy about that. They can be in the backyard when the weather's nice, and I can make a spot in my sunroom for them and install a dog door. The mamas can go in and out when they need to. I've been wondering what to do when I retire this fall. I may have found my calling."

"Really?" *I love this idea.* "That is so cool."

"Yes, it is, isn't it?" she said with pride. "These puppy mills are a bad deal. Cindy said a lot of these dogs are super inbred and have lots of medical problems, but we won't know until they're all assessed. The two girls I'm taking home seem to be okay, but it's too soon to know about their babies."

I asked, "So, what kind of dogs are you taking home?"

"One's a cocker spaniel, the other's a Jack Russell terrier."

"I like both those breeds, and they'll keep you busy."

"I know. I think I'll do some more volunteer work here too. Thank you for this, April." She gave me a hug. "But honestly, I'm getting tired. Do you mind if we head home?"

We finally tracked Cindy down at the shots station.

Mom said, "We're going to take off now. Can I grab those two girls and their little ones—or do you need me to come back?"

"Please take them. They have already cleared the floor and are in crates in the cat room, ready and waiting for you. I have your paperwork with all your info, so we're set. I can't thank you both enough for all your help today."

"It was our pleasure," I said with all honesty. "We were both touched in ways you can't imagine."

"No, I can imagine," she said. "I came to the shelter for the first time when I was ten. I just wanted to walk the dogs. I had dreams of going to college to study music. I wanted to be a concert pianist. But you know what? I have a nice piano at home and a very fulfilled life right here. We're making a difference in the lives of these dogs—and people like you."

"Kind of like meeting Jesus for the first time," I responded, more to myself.

She smiled, "I have used the same analogy. Dogs have that

same unconditional and forgiving love. We can learn so much from them."

Mom said, "Amen to that, sister."

We gave and got hugs, and Mom and I picked up her new borders. Then, we drove to the pet store for beds, food, a dog door, and a gate. We found the tools we needed in her garage. I don't think she had been in Dad's shop since he got sick.

We were both exhausted by the time we got everything set up for the doggy families. Mom named the buff-colored cocker Molly and the Russell Maggie.

Molly had three little ones. Maggie had four. *Quite a crowd.* The vet figured Maggie's pups were two weeks old, but Molly's pups were only one week. *Busy months ahead for Mom.*

I felt sore as I crawled into bed that night, but I knew I had accomplished something worthwhile. I wondered what Steve was doing, and I said a prayer for our marriage.

THAT SUNDAY MORNING AS I was getting ready for church, I called Mom. "How was your first night?"

"Everyone's doing well. The girls already learned about the dog door. The tile floor in the sunroom will be easy to clean, which is good because house-training will be a huge task. Maggie acts like having grass under her feet is uncomfortable."

"That's so sad," I replied.

"I know, but she'll adjust. She has a better life ahead of her."

I hung up and headed to church. The pastor talked about forgiveness, letting go of past sins, and moving forward. *Just what I need to hear.*

10

I was surprised to find Steve there when I got home. He generally didn't get home until late afternoon on these "weekends away." I greeted him with a big smile and a kiss. "Hey, baby. Fancy meeting you here! How was your weekend?"

"Fine," he replied. "And yours?"

I started to tell him about the day at the animal shelter with my mom, but he interrupted, "You know what, this story sounds like it's going to take a while. Let's go for a ride. We can talk in the car. Brody, you want go?"

Brody jumped up and barked as we headed for the door.

Steve stopped. "Wait … let's grab water for us all, and we'll throw in a quick hike."

We loaded up the SUV, headed to our first hiking spot, and hit the trail. On the way, I told him about the volunteers at the shelter, the puppy mills, and Molly, Maggie, and the puppies.

On the way home, he reached over and grabbed my hand. "I haven't seen you this jacked up about anything in a long time."

"I know. I have felt so energized all day. It's been an amazing weekend. I feel like I made a difference. Know what I mean?"

"I'm so proud of you, April." He kissed my hand. "You are an incredible woman. I wish I could have been there with you."

"Me too. Those poor dogs. Cindy told us some of them don't make it. How sad is that?"

"Can we stop by your Mom's so I can meet Molly and Maggie?"

"Of course. I'd love to check on them."

I grabbed my cell phone and called to make sure Mom would be home.

When we got there, Brody met the girls in the backyard, and they got along fine. Then, Brody checked out the new space. With him wandering around, the girls did too. When the pups made noise, Brody stuck his head in the dog door. He couldn't fit through it, but he kept cocking his head from one side to the other. It was so cute. We all laughed. We eventually took the girls back to their babies. Brody smelled them and then followed us to the kitchen table.

Mom said, "Steve, April tells me you guys have been doing some fishing and camping lately. Need another dog?"

We all laughed again.

I said, "Give the poor things some time to grow up!"

"No way." She waved us off. "I'll get too attached if I don't start finding them homes now. Two dogs I can handle—but not nine!"

I had to ask, "You plan to keep the girls?"

"Yeah, I probably will. I knew it might be that way when I said yes to fostering them. They've already captured my heart. By the end of next week, I'm sure I'll be hooked!"

"Brody captured our hearts immediately," Steve added.

The phone rang, and Mom got up to answer. "It's June," she mouthed. She offered her a puppy too.

ON WEDNESDAY, JUNE CALLED WITH the news. "I'm pregnant!"

They had been trying for over a year and had begun to get discouraged, so it really was great news.

When I hung up the phone, I said, "Well, my mother finally gets her grandchildren. June and Larry are expecting. She's only done the home pregnancy test, but she'll call her doctor tomorrow and get an appointment."

"Good for them," Steve said. "What about you? Do you want kids?"

"Yes, I would like kids."

"I'm still not sure. I mean, we're doing okay on our own, right?"

"Are you telling me you don't want kids?"

"It's just that you see so many divorces and fights over the kids. Who gets what holiday? Who pays for what and when? Seems so, I don't know, vile. Families are supposed to be a good thing, but that seems to be the exception and not the rule. Look at your folks: perfect marriage, two kids, nice house in town, same jobs forever. They're so settled, so steady. Then look at my folks. My father is married to his fourth wife. My mother gave up trying and lived with the past two guys. She's single now, but I fear she's just 'in between men.' The whole thing's disgusting."

"But look at your sister," I said. "Karen and Adam have been married for what—ten years now—and have two kids. They're doing okay, right?"

"I still have a lot to think about. What if I'm not good parenting material?"

"I have to ask," I replied. "Why all the talk about this lately if you're so unsure?"

"I told you about Noah. His wife is due any day now. It just put it in my mind."

I understood. That's where we left it—again. At least he is thinking. At twenty-eight, my biological clock isn't ticking too loud—yet.

THURSDAY NIGHT, WE WERE SITTING at the dinner table, and Steve said, "You want to go camping again this weekend?"

I grinned. "I'd love it. Where to?"

"Up north by Noah's cabin. The lake is beautiful, and there are camping spots you can drive right up to. It's not *too urban.* You know you're in the country, but they have little grills and toilets on-site."

I shook my head. "Sounds a little too civilized for my tastes. No lions and tigers and bears?"

He laughed. "I'll see what I can scare up for you. I think you'll like the area. I know Brody will."

After dinner, we got everything ready and most of it packed and ready to go in the shop. All I had to do was pick up some grub. We made our list before going to bed.

When I got home from work and the store on Friday, Steve was loading up the car. Brody watched us both. When Steve grabbed the dog dishes and leash, Brody perked right up.

When we were done, Steve turned to Brody and waved his arm as he opened the front door. "Load up."

Brody didn't have to be told twice. He was waiting by the car by the time Steve got there. I locked up the house, and we were off.

It was a two-hour drive. The lake wasn't that big, but the

campsites were nice. They had cleared out a few trees, and there was enough space for a rig and a boat or a camper. You could see your neighbor, but you weren't camping right on top of them. For urban camping, it wasn't bad. There was an outhouse at each end of the camp, and every site had its own grill and a water spigot that said "non-potable water." We brought our own drinking water, but having wash water was a nice bonus.

We set up with enough evening light to cook bratwursts on the grill. I had a couple of tennis balls in the car for Brody, and we played a little fetch. He loved it. We even taught him to "bring it to Dad" or "bring it to Mom," and he'd bring the ball to Steve or me as commanded. He was a smart dog and a lot of fun.

The next morning, I awakened to the sounds of birds chirping and the smell of brewing coffee. I sat up in bed and stretched. I grabbed my knees and sat there for a few minutes. *This feels so right. My marriage is good. My life is good. All my suspicions of an affair are not reality. Just unhappiness in my heart making up reasons. I am going to do what my mom and I talked about: work on my marriage. I am going to make sure my husband knows how much I love him every day. If there is another woman, that's on her. But today, he is all mine—and I plan to enjoy it.*

I grabbed my purse and retrieved my Bible. *I might not be going to church this weekend, but I am definitely going to spend time with Jesus.* I read a few verses in Ephesians before getting dressed.

As I exited the tent, I watched Steve staring out toward the lake. He looked so serene that I hated to break the moment. He turned toward me as I reached the picnic table, headed back to the fire, and poured me a cup of coffee. He kissed my forehead. "Good morning, beautiful."

"Good morning to you." I smiled in return. "I think you like making camp coffee. You sure do a good job."

"There's just something about the smell of fresh coffee brewing with all the smells and sounds of nature around." He sighed. "I love it."

"Me too." I stood next to him and looked out over the lake. "Hey, where's Noah's cabin?"

He pointed to the opposite corner of the lake. "At that end. You can't see it from here. It's nice. I doubt they'll be there this weekend with the baby due any day."

We wrapped our arms around each other and watched the world wake up.

Brody entered camp and sat beside us. *This would make a great picture. How peaceful and perfect. I am so in love with my life.*

I fried potatoes and scrambled eggs for breakfast. We decided to get in some early morning fishing, so Steve got the gear ready while I cleaned camp. We each found a spot on the shore and cast a line. Brody sprawled between us as the ducks in the middle of the lake quacked at each other. Very Norman Rockwell-esque.

"Hello, folks," we heard from behind us.

Steve and I both turned.

A fisherman with his pole and gear said, "I'm just coming behind you. Wanted to make sure you and your dog knew I was here."

Steve greeted the man. "Brody's a good dog."

Brody got up and checked out this newcomer.

The guy gave him a rub and a pat. "I was going to fish down shore a bit. Okay with you?"

"Sure thing," Steve replied. "Plenty of room."

Mr. Fisherman walked ten yards or so and started setting up. Brody tried to follow him, but we called him back. We returned to our own fishing. I heard the zing of his line going into the water and the plop of his bobber.

Just that quick, Brody was in the lake headed toward the bobber. He was going for the "ball." I tried to yell at him, but he splashed as he swam and couldn't—or didn't want to—hear me. I turned to Steve. I know we were both worried about a fishhook versus dog scenario.

"Steve, whistle for him," I screamed.

Steve put his fingers to his mouth and did one of those loud, piercing whistles I have always wished I could do. That got Brody's attention. He turned and looked, less than ten feet from the ball. We both called him back. He took one more look at his target and returned.

Brody came onshore beside us and shook. We both got rained on by the water spray and tried to turn from it best we could.

Mr. Fisherman reeled in his line and packed up to head farther down the shore.

"Sorry about that," I said with a wave.

"No problem." He waved back.

Steve and I looked at each other.

Steve said, "Who would have thought he'd do that?"

"He does like to play fetch."

Brody obviously found no humor in us ruining his game. He found some grass and plopped down with a groan.

"Poor guy," Steve said.

"I guess it's one more thing we need to teach him."

"But that was funny. Only because he didn't get hurt."

"I was worried the old guy was going to reel in too soon. Then Brody would have to chase the ball, and we'd have had some real trouble on our hands."

"Exactly! I could see bad written all over that. At least we know he responds to a whistle."

"We'll put that in our 'Brody book of knowledge.'"

We fished for a couple hours and then took Brody for a hike. We headed toward the end of the lake and could see Noah's cabin, but no one was there. Steve showed me around the outside and told me about the loft and the way the house was set up. We stood on the covered deck that faced the lake. It was a beautiful getaway.

Steve told me what he knew of the history of the place. It had been in Noah's family for years. His grandfather had built it when he was a young and newly married man. They lived there until the kids were old enough for school and then moved closer to town. It became a vacation spot for the family.

Noah's Dad remodeled years ago. The cabin had just come into Noah's hands. He wanted a few more modern conveniences, so Steve and the guys helped him out. Each generation had put its own mark on it. I could tell Steve was impressed too. For a guy like Steve, with such a dysfunctional family, that type of legend and history really meant a lot.

Back at camp during dinner, two of the neighbors came over and introduced themselves. Joe and Ellie sat by our fire and chatted for a while. We relaxed and visited, and Brody stayed close to camp. He seemed to know that home was wherever his people were.

11

Sunday morning, I could hear Steve brewing coffee by the fire. I grabbed my Bible, exited the tent, and joined him. "Good morning," he said with a kiss as he handed me a cup of coffee.

"You're spoiling me." I grabbed the cup with both hands.

"Yeah, don't get too used to it."

I sat at the picnic table, opened my Bible, said a prayer, and started to read. The next thing I knew, I heard a voice over my shoulder as Steve joined me at the table. "What are you reading?"

"Ephesians," I replied.

"Okay, whatever that means. What are you reading?"

"The book of Ephesians … it's in the New Testament. It pretty much has all the answers to life. It tells you how to treat your spouse, your kids, your boss. But right now, I'm in Chapter 3. I'll start with verse fourteen. Listen to this:

> *For this reason, I bow my knees to the Father of our Lord Jesus Christ, from whom the whole family in heaven and earth is named, that He would grant you, according to the riches of His glory, to be strengthened with might through His Spirit*

in the inner man, that Christ may dwell in your hearts, through faith; that you, being rooted and grounded in love, may be able to comprehend with all the saints what is the width and length and depth and height – to know the love of Christ which passes knowledge; that you may be filled with all the fullness of God.

"Wow," Steve responded. "Deep stuff. I like it."

Bark, bark, bark!

We both turned to look. Mr. Fisherman walked by with his pole over his shoulder and a bobber on his setup. We called Brody back. He sat down by us, but closely watched Mr. Fisherman.

"We better play fetch with this guy," I said, "so he doesn't attack all the fishermen on the lake."

Steve cooked some breakfast while I took Brody to an open area. He played until my arm gave out and his tongue hung out. He would have gone longer if I'd let him.

When we got back, I prepared Brody a clean dish of water and then washed up at the spigot. Steve served scrambled eggs and bacon with bread and butter and coffee. Steve didn't bring up the Bible again, but I could tell it had been moved from where I left it. I wondered if he had read some while I was gone or just pushed it away. I prayed for the former.

We fished the morning away and each caught a couple to grill fresh for lunch. It was a beautiful day, but we decided to head home. We wanted to relax before getting ready for work on Monday.

On the road, we made small talk about our weekend. *Nice and casual.*

About an hour from home, Steve grabbed my hand and

looked me in the eye before turning back to the road. "I know I don't say it often, April, but I do love you."

My heart jumped in my chest. It was like I was hearing those words for the first time. "Oh, Steve, I love you too." I smiled back at him.

The rest of our trip home was quiet but a comfortable silence. I felt at peace.

MONDAY AT WORK WAS KIND of crazy. Mindy, my coworker, was crying at her desk when I arrived.

I dropped my purse at my desk. "What's going on, Mindy? What's wrong?"

She tried to straighten up and wipe her eyes. "I'm sorry. I forgot you like to come in early. I thought I'd have it together before anyone else got here."

I pulled up a chair next to her. "We're the only two here, for now. How can I help?"

Tears spilled down her face again. "Joe, my husband, he left me. He's been having an affair. It's been going on for two years! Two years, April! How could he? How could I not know? Looking back, I see all the signs now. But at the time, he gave me excuses, and they seemed real, logical. He was such a good liar. We even talked about having another child. What will I tell my son? What am I going to do?"

She blew her nose, and I handed her another Kleenex.

"He's been dating a waitress he met at a coffee shop. He said she listened to him and made him laugh. We'll see how much laughing is going on by the time my lawyer gets through with him!"

"You already have a lawyer?" I asked in shock.

"Well, no, but I will. Oh, April, I still love him. It just hurts so bad. I didn't say anything to Joey when I dropped him off at school. Joe said he'd call me later to talk things out, but he's not coming home again." She fell into my arms and started crying again.

Just then, Judy, the boss, came in. I gave her a brief synopsis of the situation, and she told Mindy to go home.

"I have a meeting with an important client today," Mindy said between sobs.

"I'll have someone else handle it," Judy insisted.

We finally talked Mindy into leaving as everyone else arrived.

I felt numb. *I convinced myself the whole affair thing was just in my head, and now I hear this? Oh, God, please help me. I don't want to be right.*

STEVE, BRODY, AND I HAD a good week. Things were on a roll, and we were connecting again. Steve was communicating better, but I still felt like he was holding something back.

Wednesday night before church, my mom called and invited us over for a barbecue with June and Larry on Saturday.

"Sure, let's go," Steve said.

I was looking forward to it.

Thursday night, Steve put his lunch box on the counter and grabbed me in a big bear hug. He held me tight but didn't say a word.

"What's wrong?" I finally said.

"It's Noah's wife. She had the baby, but something went wrong. The baby and his wife are both on shaky ground. He called into the jobsite today and said she was in labor for thirty-four hours. I don't know all the words the doctors used, but he asked us to pray. I don't know how, April. Can you help me pray?"

With tears in my eyes and a lump in my throat, I sent up a quick prayer before I responded, "Sure."

I led him to the couch. We sat next to each other and held hands.

"Praying is just talking to God. You talk to Him like you would any friend. Say whatever you feel. We pray out loud because it helps us put our words together, but you can pray silently too. I'll start praying, and you chime in if you'd like."

He nodded, bowed his head, and closed his eyes.

"Sweet heavenly Jesus, we know you are in control. We know, Lord, you know the outcome of this situation already. We ask you give Noah and his family comfort and peace as they go through this trial. Please watch over Noah's wife and child. Lord, it is our desire they come through this strong and healthy. But, Lord, Your will be done. Give the doctors and nurses wisdom as they decide their course of action. Give Noah's wife and the baby strength and courage to pull through this. Please give Noah and his family comfort and love through all this." I stopped and waited for Steve, in case he wanted to add anything.

"Yes, Lord, please help," he said. "Amen."

We didn't hear anything that night, but when Steve got home from work on Friday, he reported that things were okay so far. No bad news but a continued request for prayer.

So, we prayed together again.

I was so touched by Steve's concern for this young family. At dinner that night, I said, "Tell me about Noah."

"Well, he's a young kid—twenty-one, I think. He's Richard's nephew. He and his wife were high school sweethearts. In fact, they married right out of high school. He's a good carpenter.

Smart kid, strong. His dad's a preacher. He's got that bumper sticker I told you about. He's been talking to me about God at work. He believes that stuff like you do. He talks about those Bible people like he had dinner with them last week. It's kind of cool and kind of weird at the same time. He's like a little brother, and I feel like I need to look out for him."

"I get why this is so hard for you." I grabbed his hand and gave it a squeeze. "I'm sorry, honey. We'll keep praying."

Saturday morning, we got some work done around the house and headed to Mom's at about three o'clock. We took Brody with us.

She led us immediately to see the puppies. All of Maggie's pups had their eyes open and were moving around a little on their chubby legs. Two of Molly's pups had their eyes open too.

Mom picked up one of Molly's pups. "Aren't they just adorable? I love cockers. This is the only boy. I was thinking of calling him Captain. Doesn't he look like a Captain to you?"

Brody sniffed him but didn't seem impressed.

She grabbed one of Maggie's pups. "Russells are such funny little dogs. This little guy is almost three weeks old."

Brody tried to sniff him, and he barked or yipped. We all chuckled.

"That's a tough one you got there," Steve commented.

"Yes. Terriers all think they're tough. They say Jack Russells are like clowns. You better have a sense of humor if you're going to live with one. I can see that in Miss Maggie already. I was thinking of calling this one Rocky or Rambo."

We were laughing when June and Larry came through the door and found us in the sunroom.

"I knew we'd find you with the puppies," June said.

Mom held Rocky/Rambo in her hands. "But look at how cute they are. Are you sure you don't want one?"

"No, Mom, we're good. I'm going to have a baby. Now's not the time for a puppy."

"Actually," I said, "now's the best time. You can have the dog housebroken and trained by the time the baby comes. If you wait until after the baby, you'll be too tired or too busy."

Steve and Larry responded at the same time, saying, "That makes sense."

June glared at me. "Thanks, sis. That's just what I need!"

"I can't tell you what a difference Brody has made in our lives," Steve said.

Brody came over and sat down like he was saying, "Look at me." *So cute.*

Mom put the puppy back into its bed, and we all went into the kitchen. "How did your doctor appointment go?"

"We got to hear the heartbeat," June said. She nearly glowed.

I could see the concerned look on Steve's face, and I knew he was thinking of Noah's family.

"I'm about seven weeks along, and the doc says things are good. We decided to find out the sex of the baby when it's time. I have to be sixteen weeks along to tell. That way, we'll know what we're shopping for and have only half as many names to argue over." She grabbed Mom's hand. "Larry and I would like your permission to name the baby Mitch, after Dad, if it's a boy. Would that be okay?"

Mom gave them both a big hug. "Oh my goodness, how sweet is that? He won't know his grandfather, but I'd consider it an honor. I know your father would agree."

June and I had brought something to add to the meal. Mom made hamburgers, and Larry did the honors. He and Steve stood by the grill and talked while June, Mom, and I sat at the table in the backyard or checked on the dogs.

We got home at about eight-thirty to find two messages on

the machine. "Steve, this is Richard. I just wanted to tell you Noah's son, Paul, is no longer on the critical list. He's still in the NICU, but he's doing okay. Rachel still needs prayer. We'll try to keep you informed."

The second message was from Noah: "I talked to Richard, and he said you guys were praying for us. Thank you. The baby's getting better. Rachel still has a few hurdles, but things are looking good. Keep praying, buddy. God is in control."

Steve looked at me. "How can he be so upbeat at a time like this?"

"It's just like he said." I wrapped my arms around him. "God is in control. You can trust God."

Sunday, I got up and took Brody for a walk before getting ready for church. I left my Bible on the table and my purse in the chair, so they'd be ready to grab. When we returned, Steve was reading my Bible at the table. When he saw me, he shut the book and moved it away.

Dear Lord, please help my husband find his way to you. Amen.

After showering and getting dressed, I asked Steve if he wanted to go to church with me.

"No, I think I'll mow the lawn and see about trimming that tree. Brody and I will hang out here."

I gave him a kiss, grabbed my Bible and purse, and headed out the door.

Monday after work, Steve wrapped me in a big hug and swung me around. "She's okay! She's okay. The baby's okay, Noah's okay, and Rachel's okay. It's all good!"

"I'm so glad. I told you God could handle this."

"I know you did. This is part of why the whole baby thing is so scary. Can you imagine being twenty-one with a newborn baby and no wife? Or losing them both? It's too hard."

I said, "You do know thousands of women have babies every day without complications."

"But there are problems too. I don't know if I could handle what Noah just went through."

I looked him in the eye. "Life is full of risks, but the rewards can be incredible."

The rest of the week was quiet, normal, regular, whatever you want to call it, but when Steve came home on Thursday night, he looked bewildered—or maybe enchanted. He set his lunch box on the table, sat down, and stared at me.

I pulled out the chair next to him and sat too. "What's wrong?"

"Noah came by work this afternoon. He brought the baby. I held him. I never even held Karen's kids until they could climb up in my lap by themselves. But Noah put that little guy in my arms, and you know what he did?" He showed me his pointer finger. "He grabbed my finger with his whole fist and looked at me like he knew me or something. It shook me. It was like I had a connection with him, you know? I get it now, April. As scary as the whole thing has been—the complicated pregnancy, the scary delivery, everything—and then there he was." He held his hands up like he was holding the baby out to me. "This perfect little person with his whole life ahead of him, and Noah gets to help with all that. He'll be there to teach him and watch him and protect him. You know what? I was jealous. I want that, April. I want that too. Can we do that? Can we make a baby? Do you want to make a baby with me?"

"Steve, are you sure?" I reached out a hand.

He grabbed it and held it.

"What about all the other stuff that's bothered you? I would love to have a baby with you, but I want you to be sure."

"I know I've been riding the fence on this, but I *am* sure

now. After talking to Larry and Noah, I think I can do this. I'm still scared—but not for the same reasons. I don't want to mess up. I want to be a good dad and role model. What would we have to do?"

I grabbed a napkin and started folding it to keep my hands busy. "Well, I'd need to talk to my doctor. I've been on birth control for a long time. I know June said her doctor told her she had to be off the pill for a month or so before she could even try to get pregnant. That's the first step."

"Good. Do it." He grinned and pulled me into a hug.

At dinner, we visited about everything else—our days, our jobs. That night, in bed, I couldn't remember when I felt more in love with my husband or more romantic. The love we shared was sincere and honest. I thought about that in the morning as I was getting ready. *No way this man could be cheating on me.*

12

Friday night at dinner, I said, "Any plans for the weekend?"
"None that I know of."

"Want to hike or something?"

"Yeah, but I got stuff to do here in the morning first. The hedge trimmer and lawn mower both need some attention."

Saturday morning, I took Brody for a walk at first light. After breakfast and a shower, I started my chores.

The phone rang, and I picked it up in the kitchen at the same time Steve picked up in the living room.

A woman's voice asked for Steve.

He walked to the kitchen, covered the receiver, and said, "I got it."

I hung up, and he took the call in the shop. My heart sank. *Is that her? The other woman? Oh, God, please, no. We've been doing so good. Please, Lord, no.*

About fifteen minutes later, Steve came in the house, put the phone back in the charger, and headed to the bathroom. Soon, I heard the shower running. I kept myself busy cleaning, but my mind raced in directions I didn't like.

He soon appeared in nice slacks and a shirt.

"You going somewhere?" I tried to sound casual.

"Yeah, if I'm going to be gone too long, I'll call you." He gave me a peck on the lips and left.

This is it! Just like Mindy said—all the same clues all. The lies and even making plans to have a baby with me! Oh God, what do I do? What do I do?

I started to pace in the kitchen, but then I stopped. *No. I'm not going to sit around here and feel sorry for myself.* I decided to visit Mindy and see how she was doing. *I need some of that misery loves company stuff right about now. Mom wants me to talk to a girlfriend? Well, here I go!*

I'm not sure why, but I wrote a quick note before I left, in case I got back late—if I came back at all.

"Steve, went to visit my friend, Mindy. Brody is with me. Back late. Love, April."

I grabbed Brody's leash, loaded him in the back seat, and made plans on the fly. I hoped Mindy wouldn't mind me bringing my dog, but I felt I needed him with me.

After I got in the car, I realized I was hungry. I thought I'd swing by the café on Sixth Street. I called on my cell phone and ordered a burger, fries, and a bottle of water to pick up. A first step to eating healthier: water not soda. I drove to Sixth Street, parked across the street, walked in, and headed to the counter to get my meal when I saw them sitting in a back booth.

Steve was sitting across the table from a beautiful woman. They were laughing and talking. She put her hand on his arm in an intimate way. It literally made my stomach churn. I ran out of the restaurant without my food and sat in the car for a few minutes.

Oh Lord, what did I just see? What more proof do I need? It's true! It was all true. He is seeing someone else. He told me he loved me, and he said he wanted a baby with me! He made love with me last night! Then today, she calls him, and just like that, he up and leaves me. He goes running to her beck and call! Thinking it was a possibility was one thing, but seeing it with my own eyes is another. No more speculation. I have the proof. I saw it!

I sat there for a while before I stopped shaking. Brody's movement in the back seat brought me back to reality. I couldn't stay there forever. I wiped my eyes, took a deep breath, and started my car. I pulled into my lane and started driving. I didn't even know where I was headed at first. I finally decided what to do, but first I needed water. I pulled into a gas station and got myself a bottle of water.

I looked at Brody and said, "I know where I need to go right now. Let's go for a hike at God's Elbow."

I felt God there before, and I need to feel Him now.

About one o'clock I pulled into the parking lot and stopped at the spot closest to the trailhead. I let Brody out, put my phone in my purse, and tucked it out of sight under the front seat. I grabbed my water bottle, locked the car, put the keys in my pocket, and headed out.

I left Brody's leash in the car and let him run free. As I walked, I talked to God, arguing with Him and myself. *Did I really see what I saw? Could there be any other explanation? Could it have been something totally innocent? If so, why didn't Steve tell me? Why would he leave to go see another woman and not offer me some sort of explanation? Why? Why? Why?*

So many questions ran through my head, and there were no answers. I cried. I screamed. I ranted and raved. And I prayed. I think I scared away every bird in the forest.

I reached the lake, exhausted, mentally and physically. Before I realized it, I woke up on the ground by the fire pit. I looked at my watch. *Five o'clock? I had better get off this mountain before it gets dark and cold.*

I still hadn't figured out what to do about my marriage,

but I knew I had to talk to Steve and let him offer some sort of explanation before I shut the door on us. I had made a vow—for better or for worse. I needed to know which side of that equation I was on. I got up, brushed myself off, knelt down, and gave Brody a hug. "We'll figure this out together, boy. Steve said he loved us. Let's hope it's true."

We headed down the trail. I felt tired and lost in thought, but I enjoyed being out in creation. I was finally starting to calm down, listening to the sounds of the birds and the wind in the trees. *I wish I had grabbed my jacket.*

Brody would wander away some, but by the time we hit the narrow part of the trail, he stayed by me and took the lead. It was only wide enough for one person to walk. Relieved when we finally got through, I watched Brody run up the hill to the west. I studied the slope to the right. It was less severe than where I had just passed. Then I heard a *harrumph* in front of me.

A black bear guarded the middle of the trail several yards ahead of me. Two cubs scrambled up the side hill. I immediately assessed she deemed me a threat.

I couldn't see Brody. I started backing up slowly, not taking my eyes off the mama bear. At first, she just watched me. I kept going back, hoping my calm retreat would make her happy and give her the room she wanted.

She turned to her cubs as they joined her on the trail. She glanced back at me and charged.

I knew what I was supposed to do. Drop in the fetal position. Cover my head. Play dead. Instead, I turned and ran. However, I was right at the edge of that narrow spot on the trail, and down I went. I screamed as I fell, seeing only a steep, downward slope. I clutched my arms over my head and face to try to protect myself as I bounced off the rocks. I hit bushes and trees. I tried to grab hold of something, anything, as I fell, to no avail. At some point, I took a pretty hard blow to my stomach. I don't know when or how I came to a stop because I had blacked out by then.

I woke up on my back with Brody standing over me and licking my face. I thought, *I'm alive? I can't believe it. I survived a tumble down a mountain and a bear.*

That's when I realized *everything* hurt. I was in a lot of pain. I tried to reach up to touch Brody, but the movement caused agony—and I blacked out again. When I came to the next time, I looked at the awkward bend in my arm and realized it was broken in a couple places. I tried to move again, and out I went.

I awoke to the sound of barking and growling. It sounded like a battle. Brody was in a fight. I tried to yell. I tried to move.

The next time I woke up, I felt a weight on my chest. Brody's head on me. He felt wet. He whimpered when I touched him. I saw blood. Now we were both in trouble.

Who or what had he fought? I had to try to help him, but any movement produced intense pain.

I know I shouldn't move, but what is going to happen to us? Are we going to die here? I was surrounded by trees and rocks. I could only manage a weak call for help. I groped around with my left hand and felt for something, anything, to make noise. I found a rock and tried banging it on the ground. I tried several different spots until I found a rock to bang it against. I wasn't sure how far the noise would travel, but I decided I should keep doing it to attract attention. *I'll bang my rock on another rock and call for help.*

When it got darker, I realized no one would be looking for me anytime soon. *They wouldn't even know where to start. My note said I was going to Mindy's, but I was going to call her after lunch.* Thinking of food made me hungry and thirsty.

I talked to Brody. I told him I loved him, and I promised we'd get out of there. And I prayed.

I woke up a couple times during the night, very cold, but Brody was still beside me. I petted him and talked to him. I banged my rock and called for help. *I am not going to give up. This is not how I want to die. I hope I will die as an old lady with children and grandchildren—and after my husband knows my Jesus. I have too many things to live for. This is not going to be the end of April MacIntyre.*

13

Steve later told me how frantic he was when he finally decided to make the first call.

At nine o'clock, my mother answered.

"Joyce, I am sorry for calling so late, but have you heard from April?"

"No, I haven't. Is everything okay?" She could hear the worry in his voice.

"I don't know. I went to lunch, and when I came home, there was a note from April saying she went to visit Mindy. Whoever that is. I checked the caller ID, and no phone call came in, so I don't have a number. She said she would be back late, but I thought she'd be home long before now."

"Oh, honey. I'm sorry. What can I do?" Mom asked.

"I'm not sure. Should I call the cops? The hospitals? What does a person do in a situation like this? Do you know Mindy?"

"I think they work together, but I don't know her last name. I think her boss's name is Julie or Judy."

"It's Judy, but I don't know her last name either, and I'm not waiting until Monday!"

"I'll call the local hospitals. You call the cops."

"Okay. We'll talk in an hour? Half an hour?" Steve was glad to have a plan of action, something to do instead of just waiting.

"I'll call you when I'm done," Mom suggested.

"Okay, good. Talk to you soon."

A woman's voice answered his call: "911, what is your emergency?"

"My name is Steve MacIntyre, and my wife is missing."

"How long has she been missing, sir?" the dispatcher asked.

"Well, that's just it, I don't know for sure. When I got back from lunch, I found a note. It said she would be back late, but I can't imagine her being gone this long without something being wrong. It's just not like her. I know something has happened to her. Can you help me?"

"I understand, sir, but in most cases the person comes home on their own with a good explanation. We cannot file a missing person report until she has been gone more than twenty-four hours."

"But she could be dead by then! What if she's lying somewhere hurt? Have you had any reports of car wrecks? I can give you the description of our SUV."

"Yes, sir," the woman replied. "We have had three MVAs since noon. All persons involved were identified."

"MVAs?"

"Motor vehicle accidents."

"So, what am I supposed to do?"

"I know it's hard, sir, but you just have to wait for now."

Steve hung up with some very unpleasant words for the 911 operator. His ranting and raving didn't help. He collapsed at the table with his head in his hands.

Oh God, what do I do? He looked up and saw April's Bible on the table. He thumbed through it. Tucked inside was a bulletin from last Sunday's service with phone numbers for the pastor and assistant pastor. He grabbed his phone again and dialed.

A man's voice answered.

"Hi, you don't know me, but my name is Steve MacIntyre. My wife goes to your church."

"I'm Randy. How can I help?"

Steve dove right into the problem. "April's missing."

"Excuse me? What do you mean by *missing*?"

Steve explained the situation to Randy. "I just have a gut feeling something is wrong. This is so out of character for her. I called the cops, but they said I can't report her as a missing person until tomorrow. They told me there was no one meeting her description in a traffic accident. I don't know what to do."

"Have you called Mindy?" Randy asked.

"I don't know how. Do you know her? I think they work together."

"Sorry, I don't. Most of the time, in these situations, the person comes home—"

"That's what the cops said, but I just *feel* like something is wrong."

"Can I pray with you?" Randy asked.

"What? Sure. It couldn't hurt, right?" Steve stumbled through his response.

"No, it won't hurt."

"Dear Lord, precious heavenly Savior. You know the situation. You know where April is and what is going on. We ask You to watch over her and protect her. Keep her in Your care. Bring her home safe. Lord, we also ask You watch over Steve. He needs You right now. Meet him where he is. Help him through this anxious time. Help him lean on You, Lord. Amen." Randy paused and then added, "Please keep me informed. I will contact the prayer chain, and we will be praying for April and for you. Try to get some rest. If something is wrong, she will need you to be strong when she's found. If she just got distracted at Mindy's, she wouldn't want you up late worrying."

"Okay … and thank you."

Half an hour later, the phone rang. Steve answered on the first ring, desperation in his voice. "Hello?"

"It's me, Joyce. I called the local hospitals. They have no one fitting April's description. I also called June. She hasn't heard anything from April. I also tried calling April's cell phone, but she's not answering. It was busy one of the times I tried though, so maybe there's some hope."

"It was probably me. I keep trying to call her. It keeps going to voice mail."

"I called my pastor. They have April on the prayer chain," Mom explained.

"April's pastor said the same thing. What do we do now?"

"I'll keep praying."

"I don't like this waiting thing. I know something's wrong. I can feel it in my gut."

"If you hear anything, call me."

"Of course."

Steve returned to the dining room and grabbed April's Bible. He slumped down in the living room and opened the book. He found her bookmark in Ephesians and started reading. Sometime later, he fell asleep.

AT DAYBREAK, STEVE SHOT UP, dropping the book to the floor. He checked the bedroom. No April. He called 911 again and got the same answer. He called April's mom. They talked a few minutes, but neither had anything new to report. He called Pastor Randy and tried to contain his desperation. Then he grabbed April's Bible and slumped in his chair, clutching it to his chest.

S**URPRISED** I **SURVIVED THE NIGHT,** I tried to check Brody to see if he was breathing. I tried to rouse him, but he didn't respond. I called his name, but my throat was so dry and my voice so weak, I could barely hear myself. I poked and prodded him and thought I heard a slight whimper. That was enough to bring relief. *I couldn't handle it if he died out here.*

I felt around for my rock and starting banging and calling again. *Surely someone will be looking for me today. Maybe a hiker will come up the trail. My biggest fear is the bear coming back. I am determined to live through this ordeal. I will bang my rock until my arm collapses.*

The hours crawled by, and I banged as much as I could. My hand was sore and bloodied, but I kept it up.

Bang, bang, bang.

Call out.

Bang, bang, bang.

Call out.

And I prayed a lot. For rescue for Brody and me. For a passing hiker. For rain so I could drink. That it wouldn't rain so I didn't get caught in a rockslide. I prayed for Steve. For my marriage. For June and her baby. For my mom. I even prayed that God would bring a good Christian woman into Bob357's life. Anything and everything that crossed my mind, I prayed about.

I tried to keep myself occupied and visualized what I might look like from the air. Would a plane or helicopter be able to see me? I could view the sky, so I knew it was a possibility. *I'm on my back with my right arm to my side. Brody is with me. His head is on my chest. His reddish coloring might blend in a little, but my light blue shirt will stand out against this rocky background. Hopefully, we are a big enough target, and this ledge is exposed.*

I kept telling myself rescue would come. I knew I had to stay positive. I had heard that a person can't live without hope, and I decided rescue was on its way.

Bang, bang, bang.

Call out for help.

Bang, bang, bang.

A PICKUP PULLED INTO THE parking lot at Elbow's Lake, and the man grabbed his phone.

"Hey, Mike. It's Bob. How are you?"

"Good. What's up?"

"I'm heading for a hike into Elbow Lake. Just Bo and me. I wanted to let someone know where I was headed."

"How long you plan to be gone?"

"I should be home before dark. If you don't hear from me, you know where to look," Bob said.

"You guys are search and rescue. You'll be fine."

"You're Fish and Game, buddy, you know what can happen. I'm being responsible here. Cut me some slack."

"Okay, okay. Have a good hike."

"Thanks, man. Tell Lucy hello and that I'm looking forward to another one of her home-cooked meals."

"You know the way to the door, bud. Talk to you later."

Bob got out of his truck, put the phone in the pocket of his cargo pants, and let his German shepherd out. Bo was off leash as they headed for the trail. Bob studied a car at the start of the trail, and his cop senses alerted. *No dew under the car, local plates.* Bo stopped to smell the tires and did dog things, and Bob wondered if he'd meet the other hiker or camper.

Later, as they approached the top of the cut, Bo stopped, turned toward the eastern slope, and cocked his head back and forth.

"Hear something?" Bob asked. He watched Bo a minute.

The dog had definitely alerted on something. Bo sat down in front of Bob, waiting for the right command.

Bob knew his dog's talent and trusted it. He raised his right arm, pointed down the slope, and commanded, "Seek!"

Bo scouted for a minute before he found a good way to descend.

Bob took a little longer to find a safe path. He slowly picked his way down the steep slope, sliding some, but remaining in control. He knew Bo was on a track. For what, he didn't know, but the dog certainly knew where he was going.

Half an hour later, Bob heard something. He stopped and listened. Very faint but a definite knocking. Bo turned as if to say, "Did you hear that? I told you someone was here."

"Good boy, Bo. Seek." He pointed again.

Away the dog went, slow and steady, toward his destination. They stopped at a flatland, a small ridge on the side of the mountain. The downward slope continued, but Bo was headed south on this level spot without looking back.

Bob heard it again. Knock, knock, knock. It was closer his time.

AROUND A BIG BOULDER, BOB saw Bo checking out Brody and me. He rushed up to us. "Lady, you okay?"

It sounded like screaming to me. I tried to respond, but I could only whisper, "No."

"Don't talk. Let me check you out. I'm with search and rescue. My name is Bob. Hang with me, okay?"

I started crying. "My arm's broken," I whispered.

"I see that," he responded.

Bob checked me over, inspecting all my cuts and bruises. He pried the rock out of my hand, looked at my hand, and turned it over. Then he studied my right arm. "I'll need to splint this for you." He pulled Brody off of me, grabbed his collar, and looked at his tag. He seemed surprised. "Brody? And you're April?"

I tried to nod and whispered, "Yes."

He whistled. "Well, April, we're going to get you off this ledge. I need to do some things for you first—and then I'll go for help."

I forced out the words: "Don't leave me."

"I have to call for help. I can't help you by myself. Understand?" He sounded calm and sure.

I knew I had to trust him. "Okay," I croaked out. "Water, please."

"I can't give you water," he explained. "You might need surgery."

"Please," I begged.

"Tell you what, I'll rub some water on your lips to soothe the dryness."

He poured a little water from his bottle in the palm of his hand and applied it to my lips. It provided enough relief for me to relax a bit.

"Thank you," I said.

"I'm going to get some wood for a splint for your arm. I won't be far away, and I won't be gone long." Bob told Bo to stay by me and went around the boulder. I worried about Brody, but I couldn't see him or lift myself to look.

Bob seemed to be gone forever, but he finally returned with some sticks. He worked on my right arm, talking to me the whole time. "April, this will hurt, but I need to splint your arm before I can move you. You'll also need a backboard. It looks like you've been here a while. All night is my guess."

I nodded in agreement.

"I'm sorry. I know that must have been scary. We'll get you home. Hang on. This is the hurting part."

I couldn't see what he was doing, but he was very careful, purposeful, and confident. I felt like I was in good hands. However, it hurt bad.

When he was done, he placed the splinted arm by my side. I picked it up and down. It felt weird, but I could move it without as much pain. "Thank you," I whispered.

"You're welcome, ma'am. I have to go and call for help, but I will be back. It will be okay."

"Brody?" I asked.

He looked to my right and said, "He's just over there."

"I can't leave without Brody. He saved my life," I squeaked out.

Bob swallowed hard. "I'll get him out of here too, April. I promise. Now, relax. I'll be back as quick as I can."

Bob left his dog with me. I could hear him as he scrambled up the hill, and then all was quiet again.

BOB RUSHED DOWN THE TRAIL, grabbed his phone out of his pocket, and watched for service.

"Come on. Come on. Work!" he yelled. He was almost to the parking lot before he got a signal. He dialed.

"9-1-1. What is your emergency?" the dispatcher said.

"This is Sergeant Williams. Who is this?"

"Diane. What's up, Bob?"

"I'm at the trailhead to Elbow Lake," he said as he jogged toward his pickup truck. "I found an injured hiker. She's been out here all night. I need an ambulance ASAP. I found a phone number. Please call and ask for Steve."

He recited the number from Brody's collar while he grabbed supplies from his truck. He wrapped them in a blanket, tied it with a rope, threw it over his shoulder, and headed back up the trail. He marked the way with a can of bright orange spray paint.

14

Steve rested his head on his folded hands on the table. "Okay, God. April said I can talk to you like a friend. So, here's the deal. I need my wife. I want her home, and I want her with me. I know I've been a lousy husband at times, but I really do love her. I want her back. Tell me what to do, God, and I'll do it."

He called my mom. No one answered, but he left a message. "Joyce, I'm going to all the spots April and I have hiked and camped. I'll start with the closer spots first. I have my cell phone with me. If you hear anything, call me. It's ten-thirty. I'm heading out. Wish me luck!"

MEANWHILE, BACK AT ELBOW LAKE, Bob had marked his way on the trail as he headed back to me. He painted arrows at any intersection or junction. At the spot where he headed down the slope, he painted a big arrow on the trail pointing the way. Climbing down the slope, he tied orange plastic tape to branches and bushes every few feet. When he got to the huge boulder, he painted another big arrow. As he rounded the corner, Bo was faithfully sitting by me.

"Hey! I told you I'd be right back." He lifted the rope off

his shoulder and untied the blanket. He took out a first aid kit and set it beside me while he covered me with the blanket. "I'm going to clean some of your wounds, okay? The ambulance is on the way. Good thinking using that rock to make noise. That's how Bo knew you were here. I won't move you around too much until help arrives. Do you like to fish, April? There's a real pretty lake over that ridge. It's so pristine you can see the bottom. I love to hike up there and camp and fish. Were you hiking alone?"

I tried to nod and whispered, "Yes."

"Well, for future reference, whenever you hike alone, tell someone where you're going and when you expect to be home. It's a safety measure. Are you getting warmer?"

"No," I said.

"Okay, just a bit longer. It's almost over, okay?" He finished cleaning my left hand before he wrapped it with gauze. "You're a strong woman. You can do this. Good thing you had Brody with you. I'm sure he made the difference. A long night like that had to have been easier with your dog by your side."

I knew he was talking to keep my mind occupied while we waited for the ambulance crew. *He's a very kind and patient man, but it's taking forever for the cavalry to arrive.*

THE PHONE RANG AT HOME, but Steve had already left. The dispatch officer left a message. "Mr. MacIntyre, this is the police department. Please call us right away. Your wife has been found, and an ambulance has been called."

Steve drove to the trail we hiked the first time. With no sign of my car, he took off for the next place. From one hiking or fishing spot to the next, when he didn't see my car, he circled through the parking lot and left.

WHEN THE AMBULANCE FINALLY ARRIVED at the parking lot of Elbow Lake, a search and rescue bus pulled in right behind it. The EMTs grabbed their bags and a backboard, and the search and rescue team snatched their bags and ropes. They jogged up the trail and followed Bob's markings. When they had to head down the slope, one of the search and rescue guys tied a rope to one of the trees across the trail. The lead man anchored it, and the others used it as a guide and balance. When the lead man got to the bottom, he tied it to two different trees and then proceeded to the marked boulder.

ALL OF A SUDDEN, I was surrounded.

Bob touched my left shoulder. "These guys are going to take care of you, April. I'll take Brody out of here while they work on you, okay?"

I nodded and thanked him again.

One of the EMTs threw my blanket to Bob. He grabbed it and backed out of the way, and then he was gone.

I'm not sure I can explain all that happened next. I don't know how all those people fit on that ledge, but they managed somehow. They checked me out and wrapped me up with another blanket. Lights shined in my eyes. Things poked in my ears. They put a neck brace on me, turned me, and slide the backboard under me.

I screamed in pain and passed out again.

When I woke up, I was being set down on the ground.

Someone yelled, "Are we okay up top?"

They shouted to each other and yelled commands.

I felt like I would slide off the board as they started to pull me up. Even with two guys on either side, it was a hard climb. Finally, they got me up the slope and on the trail. They walked at a slow, steady pace, but it was still painful.

I drifted in and out of consciousness.

BOB WRAPPED BRODY IN THE blanket and asked another search and rescue guy to help him. Bob and Jake carried Brody up the slope ahead of the rescue team.

As Bob shut the tailgate to his pickup, Steve pulled in. He took one look at the ambulance and my car and bolted from his truck.

Bob stopped him. "Whoa there, buddy. Wait right there."

Steve tried to blow past him, but Bob and Jake grabbed him.

"The ambulance and search and rescue teams are up there," Bob said. "There's no room for you right now. Let them do their jobs."

"That's my wife," Steve screamed in desperation. "I've got to get to her. I've got to know if she's okay."

Bob calmly said, "I'm with search and rescue. I spent the last couple hours with her. She is banged up, but she's alive. She's a fighter. I think she had a rough night."

Steve broke down and fell to his knees. "Oh God, I knew it. I just knew something was wrong when she didn't come home last night. I called the cops, and they wouldn't do anything!"

Bob and Jake squatted down on either side of him and placed their hands on his shoulder to offer comfort.

"You can thank Brody," Bob said. "I think he saved her life. From what I can tell, it looks like he fought a good fight. I think it was a bear, but I can't be sure yet. He saved her life, but it cost him his."

"Oh no," Steve cried in anguish. "No, no! They were attacked by a bear?"

"I don't know all the details for sure, but the dog shows signs of being in a fight. I'm sorry, buddy. I have him in the back of my pickup. If it's okay, I was going to take him to Fish and Game to verify my theory. I'll call you when I know more. I'm sure you'll want to ride in the ambulance with your wife."

Steve stood up and wiped his eyes and nose. "Okay."

WHEN THEY GOT ME TO the parking lot, a couple guys grabbed a gurney and put my backboard on it. They strapped me down and rolled me the rest of the way. When I arrived at the ambulance, I saw Steve and started crying. I was so relieved and so scared all at once.

Steve rushed over and reached for my hand. He pulled back quickly and placed his hand on the gurney. His face was strained. "April, honey, I'm so glad to see you." He turned to the EMTs. "I'm her husband. I've been looking for her all morning and half the night."

"We'll load her in the back. Then you can climb in and go with us to the hospital," one of the EMTs told him.

"Thank you," he whispered.

I can't tell you much about what happened next. Steve told me they radioed the hospital, read them my vitals, and got authorization to give me something for pain. They started an IV before we hit the road, and we were off, sirens blaring.

We got to the hospital, and they rushed us to the ER. As soon as they had me unloaded from the backboard, I was swarmed again by nurses and hospital staff. Steve was pushed out of the way so they could assess, do x-rays, and whatnot. They asked Steve a few questions and then sent him away. He completed the necessary paperwork and made some phone calls. He called Mom first.

"Joyce, they found her. She's alive, but she's hurt."

"Oh, thank God," she said. "Where was she? What happened?"

Steve filled her in and ended by saying, "I'll let you know more when I do. We're at Memorial Hospital now."

"Okay, I'll call June and head over."

Steve asked the nurse at the front desk, "Do you know how to get a hold of the preacher?"

"Yes, sir. Which church?"

"The Christian church here in town. That's where my wife goes, and I told the preacher I'd keep him informed. Can you call him or give me his number?"

The nurse offered to make the call, so Steve gave her some details and headed back to the emergency room to be with me.

Within half an hour, Steve was joined by my mom, my sister, and her husband. In the waiting room, Steve shared the details he had, and they sat mostly in silence. Steve paced a lot.

Finally, a doctor appeared. "Are you April MacIntyre's family?"

Steve quickly jumped up. "I'm her husband. What can you tell us?"

"Well, it's early yet, but here's what we know for sure. Her right arm is broken. We are getting that set and splinted right now. She also broke her pelvis and fractured several ribs. Part of my concern is her exposure to the elements all night with no treatment for her wounds. That could cause complications. The next forty-eight hours are critical.

"We'll be taking her into surgery in a few minutes to repair the damage to her pelvis. There are also signs of internal bleeding. Her blood pressure is low, so blood loss is a concern.

We'll be looking at that when we're in there too. Someone will come get you when she's out of surgery. She will be taken to ICU after that. Give us an hour or so, and a nurse will let you know where to go." The doctor turned on his heels and left.

Everyone seemed to talk at once.

"So, what happened?"

"How did she get hurt in the first place?"

"Why was she on that trail?"

My mom turned to Steve. "What about Brody?"

Steve sat, covered his face, and replied, "He didn't make it. One of the rescue guys told me it looked like Brody saved her life. He thinks it was a bear. That's all I know. He's got Brody's body. We'll know more later."

My mom and sister let out a gasp, and the tears flowed. Even strangers who waited for news of their own loved ones were touched by the scene.

SEVERAL HOURS LATER, A NURSE led them to the ICU waiting room and told them to wait for the doctor. That took another half an hour.

Dr. Luke Bradford introduced himself offering his hand to Steve.

"What can you tell us?"

"Your wife is in pretty rough shape. Do you know how long she was on that mountain?"

"She said she would be home late yesterday. By nine o'clock, we really started worrying, but we didn't know where to look. She said she was going to a friend's house, but we didn't know how to get a hold of that friend, and the cops said we had to wait twenty-four hours to report her as missing. I don't know what time she got on that trail, but I'm told it appeared she'd been there overnight."

"We won't have all the answers for a while. We have her heavily sedated for now. Besides her major injuries, she's dehydrated. She's got IVs and antibiotics, but this is going to take time. The broken pelvis alone will keep her in bed a while. It's back in place with pins to hold it there. We also found a tear in her uterus, probably caused by the fall that broke her pelvis. She's also got several broken ribs, we had to plate and screw two of them. There was significant blood loss. We are giving her blood right now." He stopped and looked at Steve. "The damage to the uterus was too extensive. We had to remove it. We'll keep her in ICU for a while. She's still in recovery right now, but we'll move her to a room and let you know when you can see her. But only one at a time and don't overstimulate her."

Steve later told me he felt utter shock at the news. "You took her uterus? She can't have babies? We just decided it was time to have a baby!"

Mom and June sat together, held each other, and cried.

"She still has her ovaries," Dr. Bradford explained. "So, there are still options open. Surrogacy and adoption, but no, April cannot get pregnant."

"Oh, no!" Steve cried out. "How am I going to tell her? This is too much." He ran from the room.

"Steve, wait," Larry got up and followed him.

Mom and June looked at the each other, devastated by the news.

"The nurse will tell you when she's in her room," the doctor said. "But try to be calm and positive."

"What do you mean by don't overstimulate her?" Mom asked.

"Well, she may not *remember* what's being said with the

drugs we're giving her, but she can *hear* you. Don't say things that will upset her. Speak with calm assurance. Understand?"

Mom and June replied together, "Yes, sir."

"Okay, wait here. Someone will be in shortly. I know this is hard. We would never do anything as permanent as a hysterectomy on such a young woman if it weren't a lifesaving measure. I'm sorry."

STEVE WAS WAITING FOR THE elevator when Larry walked up. They looked at each other, but neither said a word. The elevator doors opened, and they both stepped in.

Steve pushed the button. When the elevator opened on the main floor, Steve turned to Larry and said, "You following me?"

"Pretty much," he replied.

They walked over to a garden area and sat on a bench in a gazebo.

Steve felt numb. He had no idea how to handle it. What was he going to do? How could a marriage recover from such a tragedy? How was I going to react? He was overwhelmed.

Larry waited in silence with him.

Steve finally said, "This is all my fault. I didn't want to have kids, so we waited. April and I talked about it a couple days ago. She was going to talk to her doctor. We were going to start trying. And now this? Now it's too late. No second chance. April can never have a child of her own, and it's my fault."

Steve raged on, and when he stopped, Larry quietly asked, "Do you love her?"

Steve was incensed by the question. "What kind of question is that? Of course, I love her!"

In the same calm voice, Larry responded, "Then you're going to have to make that love enough."

"That's easy for you to say," Steve shouted. "You have a baby on the way. We never will."

"I know, but you can't change it. It's done. It's going to be hard, but if you love her and she loves you, that's what matters. Make it work. Don't give up. She lost her dog. She lost her chance at being a mom. Don't let her lose her husband too."

Steve sat there for a while, digested Larry's comment, and finally stood up. "Let's go."

They headed back to the waiting room.

Eventually, the nurse came in. "Mr. MacIntyre, your wife is in her room now. Would you like to go see her?"

Steve followed the nurse. I was hooked up to wires and machines every which way. Steve grabbed a small chair and sat by my side. He reached for my left hand. Only the tips of my fingers were visible, but he grasped them between his hands and held on. Silent tears streamed down his face.

"April, I know you can hear me. I want you to know I love you. I'm so glad you're okay. I know it hurts now, but the doctor says you'll recover fully—and you'll be able to try out for the Olympics next summer." He attempted to sound light. "I talked to your preacher last night. He seems like a nice guy. And I prayed, April, all by myself. It was like you said: just talking. That's how I knew to look for you at our hiking spots. There may be something to this God of yours, April. He helped you stay alive, and He helped me get to you."

He sat there, held my hand, and watched me breathe.

When Steve went back to the quiet room, Mom was escorted to my room.

"Hey, baby girl," Mom started. "I love you. June and Larry are here too. And your pastor is on the way. Maggie and Molly are doing good. So are their puppies. My whole church is praying for you, and so is yours. Steve told me he asked the preacher to pray for you. Imagine that: Steve talking to a preacher and asking for prayers?" Mom kept up a soft, soothing conversation while she sat in the chair and held my hand. She talked to me about "stuff." It wasn't the words; it was the company and the voice in the room that made the difference.

IN THE QUIET ROOM, JUNE and Larry held hands—and Steve paced.

A man walked in, approached Steve, and reached out his hand, "Steve?"

"Yes?"

"I'm Randy, April's pastor. We spoke on the phone."

Relief flushed over Steve's face. "Thank you so much for coming."

Pastor Randy visited with them for a while and said a prayer with them for my healing and for the doctor's wisdom. He noticed Steve's hands shaking and said, "Steve, when is the last time you ate?"

"I don't know exactly. Yesterday some time."

"Let's go downstairs to the cafeteria and get you some food."

"But I can't leave," Steve protested.

"June and Larry are right here. They know where we are. You have your cell phone?"

Steve took it out of his pocket and held it up. "Right here."

"They can call you—or the hospital can page us. You are no good to your wife if you are too weak to stand."

At the doorway, Steve stopped, turned to June, and pointed. "Call me if you hear *anything*. If she needs me, let me know."

"I promise," she said.

Steve and Pastor Randy got in the elevator and headed to

the first-floor cafeteria. Although long past suppertime, there were still some edible choices available.

"I'm not sure I can eat anything," Steve said.

Pastor Randy walked him over to the deli section. They made cold cut sandwiches and salads. At the drink coolers, they choose bottles of cold juice and water.

Pastor Randy paid for both their meals and settled at a small table by the window, he said, "Do you mind if I pray?"

"Go ahead," Steve said.

"Lord, bless this food to the nourishment of our bodies. Bless the hands who prepared it. Thank you, Lord, for all you do for us. Thank you that April was found and is in the care of some very competent and intelligent doctors. Please give them wisdom to know what she needs to care for her and comfort her during this time. We also ask that you be with Steve. He needs you, Lord, right here, right now, more than even he knows. Help him through this time of trial. Help him to lean on You and seek You for his comfort and peace. We ask all these things in Your precious and holy name. Amen."

Steve added his own "Amen."

After a few bites of his sandwich, Steve said, "I didn't realize how hungry I really was! I'm famished!'

"They have a good deli here," Pastor Randy said. "How are you holding up otherwise?"

"I don't know. Everything happened so fast. My head is still spinning."

"Can you tell me what you do know?" Randy asked.

Steve talked and talked.

Finally, Pastor Randy said, "How did you know she would be at that lake? Last night, you told me she was going to a friend's house."

Steve took a deep breath. "When I prayed about it, I felt

like I should go to the lake. But I didn't know which one, so I went to all the places she and I fished and hiked recently. When I saw them coming down the trail with the stretcher, it was the scariest thing I had ever seen. I knew it was April on that board. Some guy named Bob told me he thought Brody saved her life."

"Can I ask what made you decide to pray?"

"April," Steve stated matter-of-factly. "She told me once that praying was just talking to God, like you would a friend. I knew I needed a friend right then, one who could do something. So, I prayed to her God."

"He's your God too, Steve," Pastor Randy replied.

"I'm not too sure I want a God like that. You know April. I don't think she's ever made a wrong move in her life. I can't think of anything she's ever said or done wrong. She's perfect. And yet this God let her get attacked by a bear, stay outside on a mountain all night, and took away her chance to have kids! I thought He was supposed to be a God of love. Where's the love in that?"

"Ah yes," Pastor Randy put down his sandwich and leaned back in his chair. "The age-old question: Why does God let bad things happen to good people? Well, I have to tell you that the answer is easier than you think. Sometimes it's a test. This could be a test for April in some way, but it could also be a test for you. Many people have to be at the lowest point in their lives before they will reach out to God."

"What could April possibly need to be tested for? She loves God. She's always going to church. She even listens to church on the radio and is always humming and singing her church songs."

"Well, Steve, everyone has room to grow. No one is perfect, but Jesus loves us all and wants us to lean on Him."

"I don't think He could love me," Steve stated bluntly. "I've made too many mistakes."

"That's where you're wrong. A guy named Paul used to hunt down Christians and have them killed. Jesus met him on the road one day and turned his life around. He became one of Jesus's greatest disciples. Nothing is unforgivable. As long as you are alive, you have a chance to turn your life over to Jesus. But don't wait too long. You don't know when you'll run out of time."

Steve managed a nervous laugh. "I don't know. Why would I want to be part of a group that hangs out with murderers?"

Pastor Randy replied, "That's just one example."

"So … *anything* I've done wrong can be forgiven?"

"Yes, but you have to ask. You have to want Him. He won't force himself on anyone. You will still have the consequences of your sin to deal with, but knowing you're okay with your Creator sure makes the trial easier to get through."

They cleared their places from the table, stopped by the trash can, and dropped their trays at the station.

"Can I ask you one more question?" Steve said.

"Sure."

"What if no one else knows about what I did wrong? Should I still ask for forgiveness?"

Pastor Randy replied, "God knows. He knew the moment you thought about it."

"Wow, that's rough."

15

When Steve and Pastor Randy arrived back in the quiet room, Mom was in there with Larry. June was with me. They visited until June returned.

"I'm headed home," Pastor Randy said. "Keep in touch."

They all stood, held hands, and said another prayer before he left.

June and Larry departed shortly thereafter.

"She looks pretty rough," Mom stated.

"I know," Steve replied. "I shudder to think what she went through lying out there all night, hurt and alone."

"I wish we knew what really happened. I guess we have to wait until she recovers to get all our answers."

"The not knowing and waiting is hard. I also have to figure out how to tell her about her surgery. What am I going to do?" His eyes pleaded with her.

"That is hard, but she is alive and recovering. You have to look to the positive."

Steve looked directly at her, emphasizing his words. "But you don't understand. I feel like it's all my fault. I was the one who wanted to wait to have kids. Now we can't. I don't know if she can forgive me for that."

"Don't fight battles that haven't begun yet," Mom offered.

"Take this one step at a time, one moment at a time. She needs you to be her anchor. She needs to know you love her and will be there for her—no matter what."

"I know." He hung his head. "I just feel like I haven't done anything right in forever. She told me she got the dog because she was lonely. What does that say about me?"

Mom moved closer on the couch and put her hand on his arm. "Steve, you have to forgive yourself. If you keep beating yourself up, you're no good to anyone. Ask for forgiveness for whatever wrong you've done. Jesus will forgive you, but you have to forgive yourself too."

"It's all coming at me so fast. I feel like I don't have time to respond before I get hit with something else. I hope there are no more surprises. At least she's here now and getting help, so she's on the road to recovery."

"Exactly." Mom gave brief smile. "Well, honey, I hate to leave you, but it's getting late. I need to get home. I'll come back tomorrow after work." Mom gave Steve a hug.

As Steve sat alone, he thought about how he got to that point. He still didn't know or understand why I had left a note saying I was going to a friend's house and ended up on the ledge in the woods. He looked to the ceiling and asked, "When will we know what really happened, God?" Then he headed to my room again.

He gazed at the machines and took in the odd little beeps, noises, and flashes of light around me. I was totally out from the drugs. No response, just there. He sat in his chair and gently rubbed my fingers. "April, I'm sorry. I haven't been the best husband. I know I've done lots of wrong stuff, but marrying you wasn't one of them. I love you so much. Please come home to me. Please give us another chance." Tears rolled down his cheeks. "Please, God."

He fell asleep by my side.

After midnight, a nurse told him to go home. He got the phone number to the nurses' station and gave them his cell phone number before heading out the door. He stood in the parking lot for a minute or two before he realized his pickup was still at the Elbow Lake parking lot. He dialed Richard's number.

"I'm sorry to call so late, but I need a favor."

Richard sounded sleepy. "Sure, Steve. what's up?"

"I'm at Memorial Hospital, and I need a ride to get my truck."

"I'll be right there."

Twenty minutes later, Steve saw the lights of Richard's pickup pulling in at the emergency room entrance.

After Steve buckled up and they exited the parking lot, Richard said, "Okay, buddy, now tell me what's going on."

Steve filled him in as they headed to Elbow Lake. Just as they finished the conversation, they pulled into the parking lot. That's when Steve realized he needed to get my car home too. Richard offered to come back with him after work one day to grab it. Steve thanked him.

"We'll all be praying for you." Richard waited until Steve got in his pickup and started it up. They pulled out of the parking lot in tandem.

STEVE PULLED INTO THE DRIVEWAY and entered the house. It was so quiet. No me. No Brody. Everything was just as he left it, which seemed odd in itself. I was always there to tidy things up and set things right, but not this time. He looked at the pictures on the walls. Our wedding day. The family picture from June's wedding. Pictures of Brody. He took one of these off the wall and sat down with it.

"Oh, Brody, how can I thank you, bud? I'm told you saved her life. I wish you were coming home too. Thank you, man. I love you."

He hung the picture back up and headed to the bathroom. He saw the message light flashing on the phone and hit play. The first one was from the police department dispatch saying they found me. The second was from Karen to check on how I was doing. The third one was from Bob. He gave his phone number and asked Steve to call him before nine o'clock or after six in the morning. Steve wrote down the number and headed for bed. He thought sleep wouldn't come since it had been such an tumultuous day, but he fell asleep quickly.

SHORTLY AFTER SIX O'CLOCK, HE rolled out of bed. First things first, he needed some coffee. Once the coffee was brewing, he dialed Bob's number.

"How's your wife?" Bob asked.

"Heavily sedated for now. I'm told she should make a complete recovery, but it will take some time. She had emergency surgery. Broken bones and dehydration. I want to thank you again so much for finding her and for helping out with Brody."

"Hey, have you got some time this morning? I want to stop by to talk about the dog."

"Sure thing. I'm at home right now."

Steve gave him the address and hung up. Within five minutes, a cop car pulled up outside the house. He let Bob in.

"I hope my cruiser doesn't alarm the neighbors." Bob pointed over his shoulder.

"I didn't realize you were a cop. I thought you were search and rescue."

"I'm both. My dog is trained for search and rescue, so when I'm not fighting crime, I'm off to the rescue," he joked.

Steve smiled and headed to the kitchen. "Cup of coffee?"

"Sure, that'd be great."

They both sat at the table.

"What did you find out about Brody?" Steve asked.

Bob started by explaining that Bo had discovered me. "I took Brody to my friend Mike. He's a Fish and Game officer. He's familiar with wounds caused by bears, mountain lions, the big animals. I don't know what all happened that night, but at some point, your dog had a fight with a bear. He then made his way back to your wife, lay his head on her chest, and died there. I don't think she knew Brody died, and I didn't tell her. I figure that's best left to the family." He reached in the pocket of his uniform pants and pulled out Brody's collar. "I thought you might want this back. Unless you have other plans, I would like to place Brody in the canine cemetery where we place our canine officers. Brody definitely saved your wife's life. He deserves a hero's burial."

"Yeah, I guess that would be okay. Is this a place I can take April once she's better?"

"Yes, of course. I didn't want to do it without your permission. Did you want to be there?" Bob offered.

"As much as I'd like to say yes, I'm heading back to the hospital shortly. I don't know how long April will be out, but I would like to be there when she wakes up."

"I understand. I'll take care of things and give you the details later." Bob stood up. "Give the missus my best. I'll be praying for her—and for you too."

"I've been hearing that a lot lately."

"Hey, you can never have too much prayer! I'd like to check in with you later ... if you don't mind. I feel like I'm connected here. I keep replaying the picture in my head of April lying there and the dog on her chest. It really tugged at my heart. I've been first on scene before, but something about that one really got to me. You can tell me to back off and go away, and I'll do it, but I'm here as a friend ... if that's okay."

Steve stuck out his hand, and Bob grabbed it. "I owe you a lot, man. You found my wife. You saved her. I consider you a friend for life. You are welcome anytime!"

They walked to the door together. "You have my private cell phone number," Bob said. "Call me if you need anything."

"Thanks. I better get to the hospital." Steve shut the door and headed for the shower. He ate a little breakfast and took off.

STEVE ARRIVED AT THE HOSPITAL just as Mom was leaving my room, and he walked her to the elevators. "She's still pretty groggy," Mom said. "The nurse reported she woke up once last night ... asking for Brody."

"Oh, no. How am I going to tell her?"

"Now may not be the right time, but you decide. Play it by ear—and don't be afraid to pray about it." She squeezed his arm and headed for the door.

I DON'T REMEMBER MUCH ABOUT Monday or Tuesday. I understand I woke up a few times and talked to my family, but I have no real recollection of it. The drugs took their toll. I'm told Steve was my constant companion during that time, only taking a break when my mom or sister came in. He was told to take off all the time he needed from work, and he did.

Bob came to our house for coffee again on Tuesday, and every morning after during my hospital stay. He talked to Steve about Brody and the service held for him. They talked about fishing, camping, and Jesus. Steve was getting more comfortable with the subject, and Bob was a good source of information. He knew the Bible and could answer Steve's many questions as their friendship grew.

On Wednesday morning, Steve came to the hospital and met my mom again as she left my room and headed for work. I was sleeping. The same hospital sounds played out in a rhythm as he sat there with me. He turned on the TV and left it on a game show. He turned to the window, hands in his pockets, and gazed out at the parking lot.

I opened my eyes and looked around. I felt kind of foggy. I was sure I needed to shave my tongue. The taste in my mouth was horrible. My nose itched, and I noticed weird little oxygen tubes protruding. I thought, *Okay, I'm alive and in a hospital. That's good.* I saw a splint on my arm. My left arm had tubes, and my right hand was wrapped up like a mummy. I could hear beeps and swooshing sounds. I saw Steve at the window with his back to me. *He's here!* As soon as the scene in the restaurant played through my head, I said, "I know about your girlfriend." I admit it was probably an incoherent squeak.

He spun around as I croaked out my sentence. He was by my side in flash, gushing all over me. "April, you're awake! Thank you, God! I have been so worried. I'm so glad you're alive. I'm so glad you're okay."

The more he talked, the madder I got. "Water please."

"Okay. I'll be right back." He rushed out and returned with a nurse.

She checked me out, took my vitals, and asked me a few questions.

I knew my name, the year, and the president. I guess that meant the brain bucket was in working order. She said she'd get me some ice chips and left the room.

Steve huddled by my side. "Oh, honey, I'm so glad you're okay. I have so many questions, but we'll wait until you're ready to talk."

The nurse returned with a cup of ice chips and a spoon. She told Steve to introduce it to me slowly. She gave me a little on the tip of the spoon before handing the cup to Steve. "Help her with this whenever she asks. Okay?"

"I promise." He crossed his heart and held up two fingers like a Boy Scout pledge.

The nurse nodded, looked at me again, and left.

I took a couple spoons of ice and then said, "No more."

Steve held my fingertips again.

"I know about your girlfriend," I plainly stated.

He quickly pulled his hand up and looked away. "When … when did you find out?"

"I saw you with her."

He looked me straight in the eye, and I could see the confusion. "What do you mean you saw me with her? When?"

"Right before I went to God's Elbow. I saw you two at the café."

"I was with Denise at the café." He still looked confused.

"I don't need to know her name. It's bad enough you cheated on me." My voice was still weak, but I had to get it out. *I have to do this now.*

"April, I don't understand. I went to lunch with Richard's wife, Denise. She was asking me to build a display case for Richard as a birthday present. I was back home by one-thirty.

You and Brody were already gone. Denise is not my girlfriend. Never was, never will be. What you saw was totally innocent."

"Then why didn't you tell me where you were going?"

"I don't know. I guess I got so used to not telling you things. I just left and didn't think about how it would look to you. Oh, April, I'm sorry. Is that why you went to the lake and not Mindy's … because you saw me with Denise?"

I nodded.

"Then this is doubly my fault." He ran his fingers through his hair and started pacing. "Man, oh, man. I'm such an idiot. I'm so sorry. I really am. Please forgive me. Please give us another chance." He sat and reached for my fingertips again.

I confronted him. "What did you mean when you asked me how I found out? There was a girlfriend, wasn't there?"

He hung his head again. He took a deep breath. His shoulders sagged in shame, but he looked me in the eye. His voice was very quiet. "Yes, there was. She was the architect for this project. It started a few months ago. We had to go over some plans, so we had lunch together a few times. And then a few dinners. I justified it at first. We had to take care of the details, so it made sense to do it while we ate. But one thing led to another. I know it was wrong. I know it. And I am more sorry than you will ever know." He held my gaze with his.

I could see the pain and anguish there, but I wasn't letting him off the hook that easy. Not yet. We were in this too deep. I had to know, so I confronted him. "Did you sleep with her?"

"Oh, honey—"

"Did you sleep with her?"

"Yes. Twice," he admitted.

I closed my eyes and pushed my head into the pillow. I hated him. I really hated him at that moment, but I promised myself, my mother, and my Jesus that I was going to fight for my marriage. Somehow, I had to keep going.

"Did she know you were married?" I whispered without raising my head or opening my eyes.

He simply replied, "Yes."

My mind raced a hundred ways. I wanted to hit, scream, punch, and fight, but I was hurting all over and didn't have the energy.

"And the overnight weekends, were they with her?" I wanted to know—I needed to know—the whole truth.

"What?" He genuinely sounded shocked. "No! I told you where I was going and what I was doing. Seriously, April. I wouldn't lie to you like that!" I think he understood how unbelievable his words were right then because he calmed right down.

He continued, "You're right. It does sound stupid when I say it like that, but I *was* with Richard and Noah on those weekends. These are the guys who have been talking to me about your Jesus. They have been preaching to me up one side and down the other. They're part of the reason why I broke it off with Jackie. They told me I was messing up. They talked to me about all kinds of stuff. Hanging out with those guys helped me see what an idiot I had become. The day you and Brody got skunked and I called your office, I totally lost it. I knew you were fine when I left home. When your boss said you called in sick, I could hear the laughter in the background. I thought you were leaving me. I couldn't get home fast enough. It made me realize I had best get my head on straight.

"When I thought I was losing you, I realized how much I didn't want to lose you. I broke it off with Jackie for good. Then when she called the house that day before we went hiking, I realized what a manipulator she was. I talked to Richard about it the next day. Her firm had her pulled from the job."

He stopped and took a breath. "Look, I know I did wrong. I know I'm the lowest form of scum, but I also know I love you and don't want to lose you. Please say you'll give us another chance. You are my soul mate. You complete me. Please don't leave me."

His comment about soul mate hit my heart hard. I wasn't any better than he was. According to the Bible, if you think about it, it's the same thing as doing it. And I thought about Bob357. Tears rolled down my cheeks. I needed to confess too. I mulled it all over, and then I started right in.

"I signed up on that dating site findmysoulmate.org, and I met a guy on there. We never met. We only chatted online. It was because of my conversations with him that I got Brody. He's the one who recommended I take a fishing class. In fact, my contact with him brought us closer together. I deleted the account, but I cheated too. What I did was just as wrong. I'm scum too. I need you to forgive me."

"Oh, honey. It's okay—"

"It's *not* okay. None of this okay. How can we love each other and cheat on each other? We need to fix this now, or we'll never make it."

He nodded, placed my fingertips between his hands, and said, "You're right. What should we do?"

"I don't know." I was beyond tired. I pushed back into the pillow again. "Water please."

He spooned more ice, and it dissolved as I thought about our situation. *I don't hate him. I don't want to live without him. But can we rebuild? Can we trust each other again? Will I wonder if he is cheating again every time he is late? Oh Lord, what should I do?*

"I'm tired," I finally said.

"Okay, you rest. I'll be right here." He set the cup down on my table, and I drifted off to sleep again.

WHEN I WOKE UP, STEVE was gone. June was in the chair by my bed with a magazine. "Water please," I said.

"Sure, sis. Hang on." She spooned the ice chips and water for me.

"Are you okay?" I asked. *She is pregnant and dealing with the stress of being at a hospital bedside. That can't be good.*

She laughed. "Only you would ask me that at a time like this! You're incredible."

"I'm sorry to put you through this. The baby—"

"The baby will be fine. I'm sitting in a chair, not kickboxing."

"But stress isn't good for you during pregnancy," I offered.

"Really, Dr. MacIntyre? I appreciate the consult, but I'm good. Now, you, on the other hand, I *am* worried about."

"Sorry." I swallowed and requested more water.

"So why were you on that trail? Steve said something about going to see a friend, and then they find you in the mountains. What's up with that?"

I had to smile at her. *Only a sister can confront you on your deathbed! Okay, that is a little dramatic, but seriously, I am not getting any pity from this girl.* I turned my head to look her in the face and asked, "Truth?"

"I dare ya."

I smiled. *Just like when we were kids.* I dove right in. "I saw Steve in a restaurant with another woman. I thought he was cheating on me. I took a hike to clear my head and met a bear on the way back down."

"You were attacked by a bear?"

"No, more like confronted. I fell off the mountain as she was making her charge. She had cubs with her."

"Oh, April, how scary! They say you were out there all night. Is that right?"

"Yeah." I had to think about when I left, and I remembered looking at my watch. "It was after five o'clock when we left the lake."

"You're lucky to be alive on two levels. You beat the bear and the mountain."

"No, Brody beat the bear. I heard them fighting. He came back and lay down with me. He had blood on him. I don't know if it was his or the bear's."

"That is so sad." She changed the subject while offering me more ice. "Mom's been here every day. She'll be back later. You've been asleep most of the time. Some guy took Steve out to get your car from the lake. He'll be back shortly."

"How's Brody?"

"Would you like more ice?" She raised the cup and spoon. I took the offer and let it melt. *She is avoiding the subject. Too obvious.* "Where's Brody?"

"Look, April, I don't want to do this part. Okay, I know how much you loved that dog, and it's just not fair. I can't do this." She got up and ran from the room.

She said "loved." I know that's what she said. Not "love" but "loved." I know my dog is dead. He fought that bear and saved my life. And that is one more reason to be mad at Steve. But I can't do that. I was the one who jumped to conclusions in that café. I was sure that what I saw was Steve with his girlfriend. I was wrong. Okay, according to Steve, I was wrong. Oh, God, how do I sort this out?

I pushed my head into the pillow and prayed. *Only God can untangle this web.*

16

I must have drifted off again because the next thing I knew, they were taking vitals again. I could hear and feel the nurse moving around. I opened my eyes and watched her.

"Hello, April. How are we feeling?"

"Well, *this* part of *we* feels like it lost a fight with a mountain. What about your part?"

She laughed. "Good. A sense of humor will help you heal. Don't lose that. Never take life too seriously. You only get one shot at it; you might as well enjoy it."

As I was trying to decide if she was being profound or flippant, Dr. Bradford came in the room. He was tall, dark, and handsome, like a TV doctor, but there he was in the flesh—and here I was at my worst. I had to smile at my own joke.

"How are you feeling today?" he asked.

The nurse replied, "She tells me she feels like she lost a fight with a mountain."

"I bet she does." He checked under my blanket and felt my legs and feet. I had those things on my legs that inflate and deflate to keep the blood circulating. I could constantly hear the sounds.

He checked my computer chart. "Can we talk?"

"You bet, Dr. Luke. Whatcha wanna know?"

He smiled. "Tell me what happened on that mountain."

"I was walking down the trail and met up with a mama black bear and her two babies. She took umbrage to sharing the trail and charged me. I turned to run and tumbled off the side of the mountain."

"And you were there by yourself, all night?"

The pain of loss hit me. "My dog was with me."

"Here's the deal. You broke your pelvis in that fall. We had to do surgery on you. You have some new hardware that will make airport security a challenge—and probably an embarrassment." He waited like he expected questions, and then he plunged ahead. "We had to remove your uterus." He let that sink for a moment, and I needed it.

I turned my head away, stunned by the news.

He placed his hand on my arm in a comforting gesture, and the truth dawned in full force: *No babies for me.*

"I know this is hard, but we had no choice. There was a tear in the uterus that must have occurred during the fall. Then you lay there all night with a slow bleed. The two things combined left us with no choice. There was no way to save it. I am so sorry. We did not remove your ovaries, so you will have options. You can always use a surrogate or adopt. You and your husband can discuss that later."

I said, "Does he know?"

"Yes. I told him when I finished operating on you." He noticed my tears. "I can send someone to talk to you."

"Thanks, Doc, but no. I need some time." *This is a lot to digest. No babies. No chance. Wow!*

"Listen, you are a strong, healthy young woman. You will heal. You will recover from this, but it's going to take a while. You'll be here in ICU for at least a couple more nights, but if you continue to rally like this, you can probably go to a regular bed by the end of the week. How does that sound?" He acted like I was nine and getting a pony for my birthday.

"How long will I be in the hospital?"

"Let's take it one day at a time. We don't need to rush this. You took a major tumble down a steep mountain. You still have swelling and bruising, and you're recovering from surgery. Let's see how it goes, okay?"

I wanted to be nice, but I couldn't help myself. "I'll make a deal with you. I'll play the 'see how it goes' game with you if you can get me some real food. How about some nice green hospital Jell-O or that broth that smells like whoever had it before didn't like it either. Can we do that?" *There, how's that for my old cranky self?*

"Ah, *Let's Make a Deal*, is it? I like that game. Okay, I'll take your see-how-it-goes attitude and throw in a liquid diet in the morning." He held up a finger to stop me. "On one condition. You're going to play nice with the doctor and nurses, okay?"

I had to chuckle. "You got me there. However, I want to know what happened to my dog." I teared up again. I had to know the whole truth.

He grabbed a pad from his pocket and wrote a note. "I'll see what I can find out."

I whispered, "Thank you," closed my eyes, and turned my head to the window. *He died out there because of me. I thought Brody came back to comfort me, but he was probably seeking comfort. Poor guy. Poor brave baby. I didn't have him in my life for long, but he sure changed my life in the time I had him.* I drifted off to sleep thinking about Brody.

I WOKE TO THE FEELING of my hand being held and my fingers being rubbed. I knew it was Steve.

"Hey, babe," he whispered. "How are you?"

I turned my head toward him. "About like you'd expect. I hurt all over—inside and out."

"I know, honey." He brushed the hair back from my forehead. "I wish I could take the pain for you. I'm so sorry for my part in this, but we'll get through this together. Okay?"

"Water please."

He grabbed the cupful of ice, spooned some into my mouth, and waited while I let it dissolve. When I swallowed, he offered more.

"Please."

He lifted the spoon. "Can I ask you a question?"

I nodded.

"Did the bear actually attack you?"

"No, not me," I shared the details with him. "I think that bear started down to finish me off, but Brody fought him off."

"That makes sense."

"Please tell me about Brody."

"Oh, honey. I'm so sorry. I am so, so sorry, but he didn't make it. The guy who found you, Bob, took Brody to a friend of his, a Fish and Game guy. He asked if they could bury him with the police dogs. He said he was a hero and deserved a hero's burial. I told him yes. He said I could bring you there later."

I let the tears flow. *I rescued him—and then he rescued me. I'm not sure how to digest that. He loved me enough to lay down his life for me. Wow, I don't feel worthy.* "Can I talk to Bob?"

"I don't know. Only family is allowed in the ICU, but I can check. How's that?"

"Thank you," I whispered.

We sat there surrounded by hospital sounds—the beeps,

the whooshing noises, the calls over the intercom in the background—and Steve reached for my hand. "I have something to tell you April, and I'm sorry, but it will hurt."

I looked in his face. *Now what? More hurt?*

He didn't wait for me to respond. He took a deep breath, gathering courage, I suppose. "The doctor told me he had to take your uterus. He said there was a tear and some bleeding. He said they didn't have a choice." He leaned back in his chair, obviously relieved that he got the words out.

"I know."

"You know? Who told you? When?"

"The doctor told me this morning. He told me he didn't want to, but he had no alternative. I can't have a baby—*ever.*"

"I'm so sorry, April." I could see his pain. "I was the one who wanted to wait, and now it's too late. Can you ever forgive me?"

I had to think about that for a minute. *The list of things to forgive my husband for is getting long. As soon as I thought that, I remembered that God has forgiven me for so many things too. But one thing piled on top of another. And another. How did anyone cope through layers of life dumping on them all at the same time?*

"April?" Steve asked.

"Huh?" I was so lost in thought I forgot we were talking.

"I was asking if you could forgive me."

"Everything has happened so fast. My head is still spinning. I need time to sort this all out. I just hope there aren't any more surprises."

"Understood. It has been a rough couple of days, hasn't it? More for you than me, but we're both on this journey."

"I need rest now, okay?"

"Sure, babe. Go ahead. I'll be right here." He leaned back in his chair, still holding my hand.

I had so many things to think about.

Steve did have an affair, but he ended it on his own.
My dog is dead. He lost his life saving mine.
And I can't have babies.

To make matters worse, my sister is pregnant, so the whole baby thing is going to be in my face. I don't begrudge June and Larry their baby, but the timing seems so cruel. Will I be able to be happy for June? Or will I be jealous of her and her baby? I want to be happy, but part of me is jealous. It doesn't seem fair. None of this seems fair. So overwhelming. It never rains, but it pours, right?

When the nurse came in to check on me, she noticed I'd been crying. "Are you in pain?" she asked.

"I'm okay. Just a lot of take in."

"Do you need something for depression? Or someone to talk to you."

"Can my pastor visit me?" I asked.

"Absolutely. Clergy are welcome if you want them."

"What about her rescuer?" Steve interjected.

She was charting something at the IV and turned to Steve. "Excuse me?"

"The guy who found her, he's a search and rescue guy. Can she talk to him? He would be able to answer some questions for her."

"Let me check. I'll let you know."

She finished up her work and left my room.

"Thank you for that," I said.

"I want you to have the answers you need. Bob might be able to help," he explained.

"What day is it?" I asked.

"Wednesday."

"Did you call my office and fill them in?"

"Of course. I spoke with Judy and explained everything. I asked her to tell Mindy too so she wouldn't worry too. Someone will cover your accounts until you're back in working order. The office wants to know when you get out of ICU so they can visit and send flowers. Richard told me not to come to work until you're in the safe zone."

"Thank you."

WHEN I WOKE UP AGAIN, Steve was gone. "He'll be back soon," the nurse said. I was glad for the time alone. *How do I go about forgiving him for everything? My head echoed with words from the Bible: "Ye who is without sin, cast the first stone."*

That was true. I had also been unfaithful. I knew God placed all sin on an even line. *Murder is on the same list as lying and gossip. Wrong is wrong, and we were both wrong. No degrees of wrong. Just wrong. Great. One more thing that didn't feel fair.*

I wanted to throw out some of that righteous anger, but I couldn't. I guessed the only way we'd get through this was one day at a time. So, with that decision in mind, I told myself, "I am married today. And that's how it will stand."

Lord, help me! Please!

June and Mom stopped by my room after supper, but Steve sat with me for most of the day, only leaving to eat. I slept off and on. He left for the night around nine o'clock.

THURSDAY MORNING, I WOKE TO the nurse checking my vitals at about seven o'clock. Steve showed up shortly after, coffee in hand and hair damp from the shower.

"Good morning, Mr. MacIntyre," the nurse said. "The doctor starts his rounds about eight, so he'll be here soon."

Steve leaned over, kissed my forehead, and sat down. "How did you sleep last night?"

"Not too bad. I woke up every time staff came in the room. Hospitals are not conducive to good sleep."

"I know, babe. Hang in there. Hopefully Doc will move you from the ICU soon."

I yawned. I wasn't in the mood for conversation.

The doctor arrived at nine o'clock. "Looking good, but you need to stay in ICU." He unwrapped my left hand and examined it. It was the first time I had seen it myself. The insides of my fingers looked roughed up. There were lots of little scratches, but the palm of my hand looked like someone had taken a meat tenderizer to it. The center was still quite raw.

"Clean and redress the wound," he told the nurse.

Steve leaned in for a good look at it and exclaimed, "How did that happen?"

"Banging my rock," I said.

"What?"

"I knew I couldn't be seen from the trail, so I found a rock and banged it on another rock … for hours. I hoped the sound would travel. That's what helped them find me."

The doctor explained, "The problem was the two rocks banging together created shards and splinters that ripped apart the palm of her hand. It will heal, but she'll have a scar there."

The doctor authorized visits from my pastor and Bob. After the nurse cleaned and redressed my left hand, I was pretty wiped out. They gave me a dose of something in my IV for pain, and out I went.

I slept through breakfast, but when I woke up, the nurse offered me Jell-O or a popsicle. I opted for the popsicle since I thought I could feed myself a little more easily. I was going to have to learn how to eat all over again until my right-handed self learned how to work a fork and spoon with my left hand. I had an image of trying to get the spoon to my mouth like a dog chasing its tail. The nurse unwrapped the popsicle for me, but holding it with a mummified left hand was as hard a task as trying to use my right arm with the cast. Steve helped me. It felt so good to be eating something. Anything!

At ten o'clock, Pastor Randy arrived. Steve thanked him and left. I was still restricted to one visitor at a time.

"Thank you for coming," I said.

He sat down in the chair and said, "I'm glad you're okay."

"I don't know if I'd go that far. I feel like the world has crashed down around me. I'm overwhelmed."

"You took a bad spill. You're lucky to be alive."

"I know. Although, in the past week, I met a bear, fell down a mountain, lost my dog, had my pelvic bone pinned together, and had my uterus removed. And … I found out my husband had an affair. I honestly don't know how to handle all this. Please pray for me."

He placed one hand on my arm and the other on the bedrail. "Sweet heavenly Jesus, we are so grateful you spared the life of our sister April. We are so grateful for the doctors' and nurses' quality care. Lord, we ask You to help her to heal physically. But, Lord, we also ask for spiritual healing. Her soul is wounded and so is her relationship with her husband. Lord, they both need You right now. Please touch their hearts and lives now. Help them both turn to You for comfort, forgiveness, and healing. Surround them with Your peace, joy, and love. In Jesus's precious and holy name, we pray. Amen."

I added my "Amen" and added, "This is so hard."

"I'm sorry, April. Trust God to help you through this. He is strong enough to lean on. You know that."

"I know. Part of me is willing to forgive Steve. The other

part wants to rant and rave and go into a full-blown rage." I turned my head to the window in defeat. "I'm too tired to deal with it. And I don't want to forgive him too soon—or he'll do it again. Once a cheater, always a cheater, right?"

"Is that what you believe? That, without a doubt, your husband will cheat again?"

"I guess so, yeah."

"We have couples' counseling at the church, and they would understand. We also have Bible studies on crises in marriage you can do at home or in a group. Given your current situation, we can figure something out."

"Thank you." I was scared and grateful. "I'll talk to Steve, and we'll be in touch. You know where to find me," I added with a weak smile.

"Yes, I do," he answered. "I best let you get some rest."

"I'm sorry. I get so tired easy. I don't know if it's the meds or the healing process, but I'm wiped out."

"No need to explain. God be with you."

I was asleep before he met Steve in the hallway.

17

The nurse doing vitals woke me up. She went through her routine and told me lunch was on the way.

I looked forward to some food, but they brought in broth that smelled awful to me. I said, "Please, take it away so I don't get sick."

The orderly frowned. "How about apple juice and applesauce instead?"

It wasn't a burger, but it wasn't broth either, so I went for it.

I still couldn't figure out how to feed myself, so Steve stepped up to my bed and spoon-fed me. The juice was good—better than water. I was surprised how quickly I got full on the little I ate. Steve was a trooper, and we got a rhythm down in quick order. I finally said, "Enough."

He removed my tray table to the counter by the sink, got a washcloth, and helped me clean my face and gown. I was impressed by his care and attention. As we finished, a cop walked by my door.

Steve saw him too and said, "I'll be right back." Within minutes, he returned with the officer and performed the introductions. "This is Bob, your rescuer. I'll go eat lunch while you guys visit." He turned to Bob. "She's only allowed one visitor at a time. Thank you for coming."

He looked like a rescuer, taller than most and built to protect. I wouldn't have known him from the day on the mountain since I didn't remember seeing his face, but I recognized his voice immediately.

"I have so many questions for you. Is that okay?" I asked.

"Sure." He sat down.

"Do you have time to talk to me? I don't want to take you away from your duties."

"Yes, ma'am. I have time. I'm clear for now. What can I tell you?"

"My first question would be how did you find me?"

He looked down at his hands. "Well, once Bo alerted me, I ordered him to seek. He hit the trail, and I followed him until he found you and your dog." He slowly brought his head up and looked at my face. Suddenly, it hit me—just like that. *I know this man. I recognize him from his picture.* My mouth went dry, and my stomach did a little flip. "Bob-three-five-seven?"

"Yes, ma'am, although I prefer three-*fifty*-seven, my favorite caliber," he politely corrected me.

"Oh, my goodness, Bob. I'm so sorry I used you, and I'm so grateful that you found me. What were you doing at God's Elbow that day?" I stumbled through my response, feeling awkward and embarrassed.

"It's okay, April. I understand. I got your last message, but I already knew you were married. Mike and Lucy are my friends. I knew when you mentioned them after your fishing class that you lived locally. I had dinner with them later, and they told me about your fishing day. Lucy also told me you mentioned a husband. I was still trying to figure it all out when I got your last message. I hope you and your husband can work things out. My wife left me for another man, and I know how bad that hurt me. She couldn't handle my job and my schedule."

"Oh, Bob, I'm so sorry. Steve and I have a lot to work through. He did have an affair. He broke it off before my accident, but there are still issues to work through. And now, thanks to my accident, I can't have babies. It's going to be a rough road, but I want us to get through it … together."

"I'm sorry to hear that, but Steve seems like a nice guy. I think he's genuinely in love with you. We've been having coffee together every morning at your house. He's very worried about you. I know he's sorry for his mistakes, and I know he wants your marriage to work."

"He told you all that?" I asked.

"Well, guys don't gossip about their friends, but I want you to know that we've been talking about Jesus too."

"Okay, fair enough. Thank you for talking to him. I'm sure this has been rough on him. I have two more questions … if you'll grant me that."

He nodded. "Sure."

"I'd like to know about Brody. What can you tell me?"

He looked down and gave his hat a spin before making eye contact again. "I've been doing search and rescue for almost ten years. When I came around that boulder and saw you and your dog, it hit me hard. I had never seen a more touching scene. It was obvious your dog loved you and wanted to be by your side. I could tell right away he was already gone. I was afraid you were too. There was so much blood at the scene, but I discovered rather quickly a lot of it was from the dog. He bled out. I couldn't tell you that day. I wanted you to be positive and hopeful. I'm sorry I lied to you, but I felt it was necessary."

"I guess we're even on that score then. Steve said you took him to someone to check him out."

"Yes. Mike is a Fish and Game officer. I took Brody to him, and we did a necropsy. He had lots of scratches and bite marks. I'm surprised he lived to make it back to you. I think it was sheer determination."

"Thank you." It was hard to get the words out. "I heard him fighting. When he came back, I petted him and felt the blood. I didn't have him very long, but he became special fast."

"We gave him a hero's burial today. Steve can take you there when you get out of here. By then, we'll have his cross up. The service was attended by every police dog on the force, half the men and women on the force, and half the Fish and Game guys. I think there was even a newspaper guy there."

"Thank you for that." I couldn't hold back the tears. "Why … didn't you tell me you were a cop when we were on that dating site?"

"I don't tell people that right away. It seems to scare women off."

"Because of your ex-wife?"

"Yes, ma'am."

"Oh, Bob, you seem to be a wonderful man. God will bring the right woman. When I was lying out there, waiting for help, I prayed for you. I'll keep praying for you."

"I appreciate that. Funny thing is, as soon I knew you were married, I began praying for you and your husband."

"So, we were meant to be friends after all. Why else would God allow you to find me on that trail? And you did get to meet my dog and my husband too."

"I'd have preferred a barbecue." He grimaced.

I smiled back. "Me too."

"So, now what?"

"What do you mean?"

"Are you going to tell your husband about me?"

"I already have. Not your name, but I told him about the dating site and how I talked to one man on there and deleted my account. I asked for his forgiveness. He asked for mine. That's where it sits right now."

"Steve and I are becoming friends. I wasn't sure what to tell him. Sometimes a rescue really gets to me. Yours was one like that, partly because I sort of knew you. Even though I do that kind of stuff a lot, I'd never come across anything ... well, it got to me."

"You were so calm and reassuring. I knew I was in good hands. You helped me, and you took care of Brody. I'll always be grateful for that."

"Glad to do it."

"So, Mike and Lucy are your friends?" I needed to change the subject.

"Yea, Mike and I went to high school together. I went into the military right out of high school and then joined the force. He went to college. We ended back where we started."

"And did they tell you about my fishing escapades?" I asked with a twinkle in my eye.

"Oh, yeah. They always have fun stories to tell about people. You aren't the first one to catch a tree, but you were the first one to grab Mike's hat. We were trying to decide if it was precision or dumb luck."

When Steve returned to the room, he stood by the door. "I'm glad you guys found something to laugh about."

Bob stood up. "Have I answered all your questions, ma'am?"

"Yes, you have. And thank you again—for everything."

Bob turned to Steve. "You've got quite the lady there. Take care of her."

"I plan to. But please come again."

"See in the morning for coffee?"

Steve nodded.

Bob headed out the door.

Steve sat down by me. "Nice guy. A regular Superman. I'd be jealous of him if he wasn't such a down-to-earth guy."

"He was awesome when he found me."

"He's definitely good at what he does. He's got a knack for it."

"Just like you," I responded.

"Like me?"

"Yeah. You have a knack for building. You are super talented that way. Look what you did with our house. We remodeled every room. You made that fixer-upper into our dream home."

"Thank you, April." He grabbed my fingers between his hands again. "That means a lot to me."

"I am proud of you, Steve. I'm still hurt by the affair—and I have a lot to work through—but I love you. I want us to work through this together. I guess the question is if you can forgive me. Do you still want me even if I can't give you children?"

His shock was obvious. "Are you kidding me? Of course, I still love you and want you. I have more need for forgiveness than you! Can we just start over? This will be a new beginning … in so many ways."

"Okay, but I think we need counseling of some kind. My pastor said they offer counseling through the church."

"I have to figure this out for myself, April. You know that. You know how I am. Please don't push me. I am listening and learning, but I haven't gotten there yet. But I'm not opposed to talking about your God."

"Okay. I understand."

"Let's just get through this week for now."

"That'll do me for now. I love you, Steve." I drifted off to sleep again.

STEVE GOT UP AFTER I went to sleep. He had been caged in the hospital all week and was starting to go stir-crazy with nothing to do. He stopped by the nurses' station and said, "I'll be back in a couple of hours,"

He headed for the elevators and the parking lot. He sat in his pickup for a few minutes and then turned the key. He headed out of the parking lot, and half an hour later, he reached his destination: the animal shelter.

He was greeted right away by a short lady with short hair and big smile. "Hi, can I help you?"

"I need to talk to a lady named Cindy."

"That's me. And you are?"

"My wife, April, adopted our dog, Brody, here a few months ago."

Cindy's smile got even bigger. "I remember Brody and April. Her Mom, Joyce, has been volunteering here lately."

"Well, I'm sorry to report our Brody died." Steve filled her in on the whole story of our life with Brody. He finished with his hero's funeral. "And that brings me to why I'm here. I hate going home to an empty house. It's going to be a while before April gets out of the hospital, possibly weeks. I miss my buddy, Brody. I know we can't replace him, but I'd like to get another companion."

"Oh, Steve," Cindy began, "I am so sorry to hear about Brody and April. That's tough, but is it too soon? Are you sure now is the right time for you to get another dog?"

"I'm not working at all this week, so I can spend time with a new dog, helping him get used to things. I'd be there all night."

"Okay," Cindy said. "I'll show you what we got. I assume you want another medium-to-large-sized dog."

"Yes, please, one that would like to hike and camp."

"Okay. Let's go back to the kennels." Cindy led the way.

Steve looked at all the dogs, one at a time, and headed back to the puppies. There were still six pups from the puppy mill confiscation.

"What can you tell me about these guys?" Steve asked.

Cindy pointed to the cage on the right. "These are about four months old. Those two are Labs, and the red one's a vizsla. They're all active dogs that would require lots of exercise and activity. In this cage, you have a Rottweiler, a German shepherd, and a pointer. They're about five months old. They're all up on their shots, but they will need to be spayed or neutered."

"Can I meet the red one and the Rottie?" Steve asked.

"The vizsla is a real sweetheart. I think you'll like her. They're good all-around outdoor dogs and are very loyal to their families." Cindy put a collar and leash on the lady in question and gave the leash to Steve. She got the Rottie out of the other cage, and they took both dogs out for a walk and into the open run. Steve watched the dogs off lead and interacted with them. He spent two hours at the shelter before heading for home, grinning at both dogs in the front of his pickup.

At home, he brought them into the yard. They ran around and played while he got the food, water dishes, and dog door set up for them. They paid little attention to him as they scouted the yard and got acquainted with their new playmate. He watched from the deck and thought about names. Finally, he decided on Ruby and Duke.

Yep, he thought. *That's it.*

He called the dogs in the house to introduce them to the dog door. They used it just fine. He showed them around the house, including where their food dishes were and beds. He decided not to leave the dogs inside by themselves on day one. So, he took them back outside, placed their beds under the deck, and prepared a big pan of water.

"That should hold you guys until I fill your new mama in on what I've done."

He grabbed his phone and took pictures before locking up and heading to the hospital.

He had some second thoughts about his decision as he walked to my room, but he thought, *If April can get a dog without telling me, I can get a dog without telling her—or in this case, two dogs.*

Steve had been gone so long that I was worried, but when he appeared with a sheepish grin on his face, it told me things were okay. "What did you do?" I asked as he approached my bed.

"What makes you think I did anything?" he protested as innocently as he could.

"Because you only get that look on your face when you want forgiveness and not permission." I smiled though. He was too cute when he acted that way.

He sat down, yanked out his phone, punched a few things on his screen, and held it up to me. "This is what I've been doing." He proudly showed me a picture of two dogs.

"They're cute."

"I went to the shelter."

"You volunteered at the shelter?"

"No, I went there to adopt."

Reality sunk in. "You adopted two dogs?"

"Ruby is the red one. Duke is the Rottweiler." He slid through the pictures. "Ruby is four months old, and Duke is five months."

"You got puppies?" I asked in disbelief. "That means the chewing stage and the housebreaking stage and who knows what all. Are they even leash broken?"

"Yes. They did good as we walked them around the shelter and when I got them home and put them in the backyard.

They'll need some supervision before we can leave them alone inside."

"Good thinking. It's warm enough out that they'll be fine in the yard. I recognize the Rottie, but what breed is Ruby?"

"A purebred vizsla. I got coupons from the shelter to apply toward their surgeries when they're old enough to neuter."

"You know you're going to have to call the vet and get them in right away so we can make them legal for in town."

"No, they've had all their shots."

"I understand that, dear, but they have to be registered in our name. They have to get their city tags and be microchipped so we can get them back if they're ever lost. And you need to buy puppy food. Brody's dog food isn't the right nourishment for them."

"Oh." He seemed surprised. "I didn't know you did all that."

"Now, *you* get to do all that. Guess what you're doing tomorrow?"

"I'll call the vet in the morning. Who do I call?"

I told him where to find the file in my home office filing cabinet. He talked about the dogs for another hour and finally said he'd better check on them. "Their first night, you know?"

It made me smile. *He is so concerned and loving toward them. I guess these will be our kids now. It makes me happy and hurts at the same time.*

18

When Steve got home, he scurried to the dining room to watch the dogs through the sliding glass door before he called them inside. They were pulling something between them, playing tug-of-war. *But what are they pulling?*

He looked around the yard, and then it dawned on him. *They destroyed their bed! Stuffing was scattered all over the yard, and they tugged the covering between them!* "It's a good thing I didn't leave them in the house," he muttered to himself. He opened the door, and the dogs turned toward the house in tandem. Stepping onto the deck, he called their names. They came running.

Later, Steve watched TV, hoping to relax, while the dogs explored the house. There was a lot of "Get off the couch!" and "Not the chair either!" and "Put that shoe down!" and "Where did you get that!" and "Stay out of the trash!"

So much for relaxing, he thought as he got ready for bed. *Puppies are a lot more work than I remembered. I hope I didn't make a mistake.* He took them outside one last time, making sure they used the dog door so they would be used to it. Exhausted, he sank into a deep sleep.

Steve woke at five-thirty Friday morning. Bob would be coming over for coffee soon. He turned from his side onto his back and put his hands behind his head to think for a minute. That's when he noticed he wasn't alone in the bed. Duke was sleeping on the bottom half of my side of the bed. Ruby was curled up on the top half, even using the pillow. Steve chortled and woke up both dogs.

"This isn't going to work, guys. April needs her side of the bed when she gets home. You can't sleep on here."

Two adorable puppy dog faces looked back at him as he got up and headed for the bathroom. The argument wasn't over—that was a certainty.

Right on time, there was a knock on the door at six o'clock. The dogs barked as Steve opened the door and ordered the dogs to stay at the top of the stairs. That didn't work, but it was a first attempt. Bob squeezed through the door and followed Steve up the stairs.

"What have you done?" Bob remarked. "Does April know?"

"Of course. She didn't fuss at me, but I do have to get them to the vet and city hall so they can be street legal."

Bob petted the pups.

Steve filled him in on names, ages, the destroyed dog bed, and finding them in his own bed.

Bob shared his own dog stories. Before he left, he invited Steve to join him, Mike, and Lucy for a camping trip.

"We're heading up to Elbow Lake on Saturday," he said. "I wasn't sure if you'd want to go there, but the fishing's good—and you can bring the dogs. I'll have Bo, and Mike will have his dogs. It'll be a break from hospital duty."

"I'll talk to April about it and let you know. I hate to abandon her. She should be moving to a regular room soon."

"Sounds good. We'll be heading up early on Saturday, but you can always join us later in the day. Whatever works for you."

Steve promised to call or text before Bob took off and made

sure the dogs were settled in the backyard before heading to the hospital.

He arrived as they served breakfast. I was attempting to feed myself Jell-O with the spoon when he came in. The slow, messy process was made easier by the smaller bandage on my left hand.

Steve gave me a kiss on top of my head, sat down in his chair, and told me about his first night with the dogs and their antics.

As they cleared away the breakfast dishes, Dr. Bradford appeared. "How are you feeling?"

"Better," I replied. "How do *you* think I am?"

He smiled. "I think you're doing well enough to go to a regular room today. How would that be?"

Steve and I looked at each other. We both said, "Good."

"When?" I asked.

"Oh, I think we can get you moved before lunch."

"Is the food better on their floor?"

"Hey, I think we have some pretty good food here."

"Will you share some with me? I am beyond tired of that soft food diet."

"I better warn Dr. Stevens about you."

Steve piped in. "Dr. Stevens will be her doctor on the new floor?"

"Yes," Dr. Bradford replied. "I stay here in ICU, but I'm available for consult. Dr. Stevens and I are in contact on a regular basis."

Steve called the vet at nine o'clock, and they had an opening if he could get there in the next fifteen minutes. He gave me a kiss and promised to be back as soon as he had everything taken care of. I asked him to call my mom and June to let them know I was moving.

Shortly after ten, the nurse prepped me for transfer to the other floor. I was still on "non-weight-bearing" status due to the broken pelvis and had to be taken on the bed I was in. I also kept my special socks that kept my blood circulating, which would be a necessity for as long as I was immobile.

My new room was one floor up, the view was nicer, and I was closer to the window. There were two beds, but I was currently the only occupant. The nurses got me settled and turned on the TV for me.

I felt an overwhelming desire to pray. I thanked God for saving my life, for giving us Brody, for bringing my husband back to me, and for the strength to fully forgive and move on. I had so many things to be thankful for. Most of all, I was thankful to be alive.

I realized I could trust my husband, and I knew that wasn't my idea. My sin nature still wanted to rail against the man. *Trust and obey? Easier said than done.*

I figured out how to make the remote control work, found a movie, and fell asleep.

Steve returned after lunch and gave me a full report on the trip to the vet. We needed to call back in a month to get their spay/neuter appointments so we wouldn't be having any puppies. They also both got a clean bill of health. "Bob asked me to go camping with him and some friends of his. How would you feel if I abandoned you for a night and took the dogs camping?"

"Go. It will be good for the dogs too. I still can't believe you did that," I said with a grin.

"I know. I can't either. I only intended to get one, hoping for another Brody." He laughed as he added, "But those two caught my eye and apparently my heart."

"I'll be fine. Now that I'm up here, I'll have a little more freedom and can receive more visitors."

He texted Bob to tell him he'd join them and let Richard know I was out of the ICU. "Tell him you'll be back at work on Monday."

"But I should be here with you," he said.

"When I get home, I may need extra help. I'd rather have you available for me then, that is, if that's okay."

"Makes sense." He started a new text to Richard.

"Oh, and please call my office and let them know I'm out of ICU and will keep them informed of my progress."

Steve walked to the window and called my office. A lady charged into my room and said, "Hi, I'm Amy. I'm your physical therapist."

"Nice to meet you, but I think you have the wrong room. I'm not allowed out of bed. I don't understand how you can help me," I replied as politely as I could.

"It's okay. You don't have to get up. We start right where you are. This is a process. Today begins with keeping your muscles toned. The less atrophy, the better."

Steve hung up and turned around as Amy lifted the sheet off my legs. She explained what she was doing and why as she did some very simple exercises. Not much, but after no exercise for a week, I got worn out pretty quick. I was glad when it was over. Amy promised to come back the next day to do more. *Probably twice a day? Oh joy!*

My mom and June came to visit after work. They were leaving when a man and woman came in. The woman looked vaguely familiar. Steve introduced them as Richard and Denise. Then it dawned on me. *This is the woman I saw him with.*

My jealousy flared up again instantly. *Forgiving is easy if you don't have to confront it. The pain is still there.* I think she interpreted the look on my face as physical pain because she came right up to me right away, placed her hand on my arm, and began talking to me like we were old friends. "Oh, April, honey! We are so glad you're doing better. We've all been praying for you!" She sounded so sweet and sincere in her soft southern accent.

Great! Does she have to be pretty and sweet? I want to hate her. I let out a bit of moan at my own disgust, but she mistook it as a response to my pain.

"Oh, baby girl, are you all right? Should I call a nurse for you?"

"No, I'm fine." I tried not to sound rude, but I don't think I pulled it off.

I looked for Steve. He and Richard stood by the bed on the other side of the room, oblivious to all else.

Denise pulled up a chair, sat next to me, and tucked her purse in her lap. "Can I get you anything?"

Half a dozen mean retorts crossed my mind, but I couldn't do it. *This lady seems genuinely nice. It isn't her fault I misjudged the scene in the restaurant that day.*

"Steve said you wanted him to build something for you?"

She quickly placed her finger to her lips. "Shh, not so loud. Richard doesn't know. I was asking Steve to make something for Richard's birthday. It's a secret."

Okay, so Steve's story checked out. "I'm sorry," I replied. "Mum's the word."

"Thank you," she mouthed. In a louder voice, she said, "We are so glad you are finally out of the ICU. Are they treating you good here?"

"Yes, I just wish I could eat some real food. Hopefully soon."

"What kind of diet do they have you on?" she asked.

"Liquid diet for now, but I'm hoping an upgrade comes with the new digs."

Denise told me about her four daughters and how long she and Richard had been together. I told her about how Steve and I met and about Brody. She was really sweet, very likable, and a strong Christian. *How cool to know these were the kind of people in Steve's life.* Steve and Richard soon joined our conversation. *I just can't hate her. Who am I kidding? I've never been able to carry a grudge with two hands and a bucket. How can I be mad at this woman?* As we laughed, it felt more like a visit with old friends.

When they left an hour later, I was quickly fading. I told Steve, and he took off earlier than usual.

At home, he let the dogs in, collapsed in front of the TV, and then headed for bed. When he retired for the night, both dogs followed and jumped on the bed.

"Really, guys?" He took off his shoes and T-shirt. "I told you—no sleeping on the bed!" He grabbed a blanket out of the closet and placed it on the floor in the corner. He showed it to them, called them over, and praised them for going to the blanket. "Stay!" he said. He then pulled back the covers and got in bed.

THE ALARM WENT OFF AT five-thirty the next morning. Steve rolled over next to two very comfortable, rather large puppies on my side of the bed. "Oh, brother. I'm really in trouble now."

Steve sent a text to check what time everyone was heading to the lake, knowing Bob would already be up. He got a quick response. The plan was to meet in the parking lot at eight o'clock.

He ate breakfast, packed, and then loaded the SUV and

the dogs. Before he left the kitchen, he grabbed my Bible and threw it on top his pack.

He stopped by the hospital and visited while I ate breakfast, and then he walked the dogs around the parking lot so I could see them from the window. Of course, being several stories up, they looked small, but it was nice of him. He waved goodbye, and away they went. I said a prayer that the Lord would bless their trip. *I forgot to ask him where they are going. I hope it is a nice spot.*

STEVE PULLED INTO THE PARKING lot next to two pickups and left the dogs inside initially.

Bob greeted him right away. "Glad you made it." They walked to the other pickup. "This is Lucy, Mike's better half, and this old crow is Mike."

"Thanks, buddy," Mike stuck his hand out to shake Steve's. "I'm sorry to hear about April. She's a trouper though. I know she'll pull through this."

Steve said, "You know my wife?"

"She took a fishing lesson from me," Mike said with a smile. "She tossed both my hat and my wife into the lake!"

"Oh, you're *that* guy." Mike smiled in return.

"Yeah, that story has taken on legendary proportions in our circle. You don't fish like that, do you?"

"Nope." Steve threw his hands in the air. "Your hat is safe with me. Your wife is too."

"Thank you, sir," Lucy said.

They all snickered and got their packs ready.

Steve let his dogs out to meet the others and grabbed his gear. Bob had Bo. Mike and Lucy brought two Labs, one black and one chocolate, Hunter and Cadbury. Steve left the air mattress at home, but he still had a pretty full pack for himself and the dogs.

They headed up the trail at eight-thirty. Steve leashed his dogs and noted the perfect weather for a hike. The trail markings were still visible from the rescue. Bob stopped where he marked the trail to head down to the spot where they found me. "Steve, I don't know how you feel about this, but I can bring you back here later and show you where we found April."

"I might take you up on that," Steve replied.

When they got to the beginning of the cut, Steve looked for signs of where I might have gone off the trail, but nothing distinguished it. He could approximate a location, but nothing was certain.

They reached the campsite and started to set up. Steve tied the dogs' leashes to a couple of trees with rope. He didn't know them well enough to let them run loose yet, so he made sure they had food and water. He got his tent up and plopped down by the fire pit.

Lucy sat beside him. "How are you holding up?" she asked.

"Fine. It's been a long week. It seems like so much more, but it was only a week ago that April got hurt … right here."

"Oh no … I didn't realize." She touched her hand to her chest. "Are you okay being here?"

"Bob offered to show me where he found her. I want to know … for my own sake."

Bob said, "Let me know when—and we'll go."

"Any time you're ready. I think I need to do this."

Mike and Lucy offered to keep an eye on the dogs, so Bob and Steve took off. They left Ruby and Duke behind, but took Bo with them. When they got to the end of the cut, they tried to discern where I might have gone over. They located some broken branches and disturbed dirt and rocks, but weren't able to look too far over the edge due to the steepness of the slope.

Finding the spot where Bob descended was easier. Orange paint still marked the trail. Bob reiterated the scenario of the day and showed Steve where Bo had gone down the slope. They followed the orange tags, and when they reached the bottom, Steve saw the big boulder with the orange marking. He scooted to the other side to the small ledge.

With no rain, the pools of blood left by Brody and me had blackened, but they remained very distinguishable. Struck by what happened there, Steve felt faint. He loved Brody too. He tried to take in the whole scene, and then he looked up and spied an outcropping not far up from my ledge. It was not huge, but it was big enough to obscure the ledge from the trail. Steve turned and looked below the ledge. The mountain continued down for several hundred feet to the bottom. He turned to Bob. "How did she land here?"

"By the grace of God. That's the only explanation I've got for it."

"And she was here all night, unable to move." The statement sounded like a question.

"I think Brody's body warmth next to her helped her make it through the night," Bob replied.

"Seeing it, being here, makes it all seem so much more impossible. She's one tough cookie to get through all that," Steve said to himself as much as to Bob.

"I know. I had to pry a rock from her hand when I got here."

19

Back at camp, Mike and Lucy were huddled near the fire pit with their dogs. Ruby and Duke hunkered close by as well, just outside of the circle, but close enough to be part of the group. Everyone was resting and relaxed.

"I got our fishing gear out," Mike said. "Shall we wet a line before it gets too warm?"

"Yeah, let's do that," Bob replied.

They all took different positions around the lake. Steve took Duke with him and left Ruby at camp. He tied Duke beside him as he fished from shore. He caught three, but two were too small. So, taking his lone fish, he returned to camp.

Everyone caught enough for lunch, and after they ate fresh fish, they decided to take a hike. They headed along the southeast end of the lake to a ridge where they viewed the lake and their campsite. Ruby and Duke did well.

By the time they got back to camp, it was close to suppertime. Mike and Lucy decided to fish a bit more, but Bob and Steve sat around the pit, got a fire going, and talked about their jobs and lives.

"My ex-wife never did like this kind of stuff," Bob said.

"I didn't know you were married," Steve replied.

"Six years. No kids. Turned out to be a good thing. She left me, claiming it was too hard being a cop's wife. It was always a fight, but my job's more like a calling for me. I told her I wasn't quitting. Finally, in the middle of a bad argument, I said, 'Let it go—or just go.' That's what she chose to do. I think I knew it was coming for a long time, but it still hurt. It's been nine years."

"April and I decided to wait to have kids, and now she can't. I'm not sure how she feels about that yet. Me neither. I don't know what we'll do. I just want us to do it together."

"Good plan," Bob said with a smile.

"Tell me about Bo." Steve called the dog over, petted him, and gave him a good rubdown and scratching.

"He was found as a puppy at a shelter. He went through training for search and rescue. That's where I came across him. I've had him for four years. He's about six now. He's helped find a lot of lost people. His count is up to twenty-four."

"Including April?" Steve asked.

"Including April," he replied.

"I'm mighty grateful to you, Bo," Steve said.

"Shall we fish for our supper?"

"Yeah, let's do that." Steve grabbed his gear and took Ruby with him this time, leaving Duke at camp.

Everyone found a fishing spot with better results. When it was time to head back to camp, they signaled one another. They had caught enough for a nice meal and added grub they had packed in. Afterward, they sat around the fire and talked about where they had grown up and whatnot. Mike and Bob told stories about one another. They were great friends, and Steve felt at home with them right away. They sat there until well after dark. About ten-thirty, they doused the fire. Steve brought Ruby and Duke in his tent for the night and kept their blanket next to his. All three slept soundly.

⁛

STEVE WOKE UP SUNDAY MORNING to the sounds of birds and other camp noises. He unzipped his tent and crawled out. Lucy already had camp coffee started. He sat near the fire, and the dogs came with him.

"That's my favorite part." He pointed at the coffeepot on the grate. "I love camp coffee."

"Me too. Mike never makes coffee at home, but he will when we camp."

"April makes fun of me for doing the same thing." Steve noticed the dogs starting to wander off, called them back, and leashed them. "Stay in camp! So, where's Mike? Out fishing already?"

"Nope. He took a walk. He'll be back soon." She grabbed a towel, picked up the coffeepot, and held it out toward Steve. "You ready?"

"You bet!" He held out his cup.

Bob stuck his head out of his tent. "Did I hear someone mention coffee?"

"Come on and join us," Lucy said.

He ducked back into his tent and came back out with Bible in one hand and a coffee cup in the other. He sat the book on the bench and held out his cup for Lucy to fill. He breathed in a big lungful of air and fresh coffee and remarked, "This is the life."

Mike tromped back to camp, grabbed his Bible, and set it on the bench across from Bob. Lucy grabbed her Bible and poured more coffee all around. "Where are we reading from today, boys?"

Steve walked back to his tent and returned with a Bible. "It's April's, but it'll still work, right?"

His friends laughed.

"Sure will."

"You betcha!"

"Absolutely."

"Okay," he replied, "but I don't know much about this stuff. I'm here to listen, but I may have questions."

Mike said, "Deal! Have a seat, and we'll start. We miss church quite often because of our jobs, so we've learned to pack the Good Book with us wherever we go. There's always time for the Savior." He sat there for a moment in thought and then said, "Turn to 2 Corinthians 5."

They all turned to the passage, and Steve got some help from Lucy navigating his way there.

They had a personal church service. Bob, Mike, and Lucy each added in their own bits. Steve mostly listened, questioning a little here or there. They spoke of tents and homes and foundations and about Jesus and His life.

As a carpenter, Steve could relate to some of what was being said. "Wait, He died and came back to life? I don't know if I can buy into that."

Lucy said, "It does sound hard to believe, but when you read the Bible," she placed her hand on her own for emphasis, "you can understand more of what we're talking about. Ask people how it changed their lives, how He helped them through tough times, about answered prayers, and how weird those are sometimes. Don't take our word for it—investigate for yourself. And read the Good Book."

Steve lowered his head. "I have a confession to make. When April was missing, I prayed. She told me I could talk to God anytime, like you talk to a friend. I prayed and asked Him to help me find her. I got this strong feeling I needed to go to the lake. So, I went to all the spots April and I had hiked and fished, and I got here as they were bringing her to the ambulance. Was that it? Was that God?"

Lucy patted him on the back. "We got ourselves a prayer warrior here, boys!" She turned to Steve and said, "Yes, that was Him. He hears our prayers. Sometimes, He answers right away, but He always listens."

"But why would He do that?" Steve asked. "I'm not sure what to believe. Why would He answer my prayers? Maybe it wasn't Him?"

Mike responded, "Because He loves you, Steve. He wants good things for you. And because April is important to Him. He considers April his daughter. He knew she would need you, so He got you here at just the right time."

Bob said, "When I got up that morning, I planned to paint the outside of my house right after church. When I got home, I started getting everything set up and ready to roll, but I got a real strong feeling I needed to come here. I tried to keep going and shrug it off. I felt bad about wanting to play hooky from my planned workday, but the more I tried to keep setting up for painting, the stronger I felt the need to leave. I didn't understand the feeling, so I prayed about it. I felt a strong urging to come, and I put everything away. As soon as I got in my pickup, a feeling of peace came over me. I prayed again for God to guide me. I planned to just take a hike with my dog. You know the rest. God brought me here to help April. I wouldn't have found her without Bo. I wouldn't have been able to save her if I didn't have the experience I do. I doubt she would have lasted the night without your dog. Too many things lined up perfectly to save her life. God takes care of His children. You can trust Him to take care of you too."

Steve said, "I need time to think about all this, but I need to tell you that I have done some stupid things. I'm no hardened criminal, but I'm no saint. I've done things I'm not proud of … things I hope April will forgive me for. Why would God want someone like me?"

Lucy responded, "Steve, God is not as concerned about your past as you are. He's interested in your future. The Bible is full of folks with bad pasts. David plotted murder so he could marry the woman of his dreams. Jacob's mother plotted with him to steal the birthright of his brother Esau. Samson was an egotistical idiot. Abraham sold his wife Sarah for a bunch of goats and some slaves because he was afraid. I could go on and on. The thing is that every one of these folks believed in God, and everyone made mistakes. People are going to make mistakes. It's how we react to them that changes with Jesus in our hearts and lives."

Steve asked, "So, Jesus doesn't care that I did bad things?"

"Of course, he cares," Mike replied. "He always cares about how sin affects our lives, but He wants us to ask for forgiveness and guidance. What better guide for your life than the One who created it?"

Steve stood. "Do you mind if I go fishing and think about all this?"

Lucy replied, "I was about to start breakfast. How about half an hour—and then we'll eat?"

"Perfect," Steve replied.

Steve went to his tent and got his gear. He grabbed Duke's leash and headed to a spot not too far down the shore. He opened his tackle box and sat on a rock. He didn't catch any fish, but he got some good thinking done. All that he had heard that morning added to what April, Richard, and Noah had been telling him. *This Jesus, He really loves people, and that includes Steve MacIntyre.*

Steve heard a shrill whistle and headed back to camp for a

hearty breakfast of fried potatoes, scrambled eggs, and camp toast. They all dished up and ate at the picnic table. Afterward, everyone pitched in to help clean up camp and then fished again. The plan was to fish until lunch and then take another hike.

20

Mike and Lucy headed off in one direction, and Bob went in another, giving them room to spread out. They had fished this lake before, and each had a favorite spot. None of them realized Steve was still in his tent.

When Steve went back to his tent to get his gear ready, he grabbed the Bible off the sleeping bag and put it on top of his bag. When he plopped it down, a bookmark fell out. He picked it up, stopped, and looked at it. On top it said "The Roman Road." It had a picture of cobbled road with verses written on it. Some were printed, and some were written in April's handwriting. Steve grabbed the Bible to put it inside, but he ended up carrying it over to his sleeping bag instead. He sat down and read them one at a time: Romans 3:23, Romans 6:23, John 3:3, Romans 10:9–11, 2 Corinthians 5:15–17, and Revelations 3:20.

It took him a while to get through all the verses, partly because it was hard for him to find his way to all the right spots but also because he was reading more than just the specific verses. He thought about each one before he went on to the next verse. It gave him a lot to think about. It was all falling into place and making sense to him.

As he was about to put the bookmark back in the book,

he noticed writing on the back, again in April's script: "1 Corinthians 13:4–7. Replace 'love' with Jesus; it's still true. Replace 'love' with your own name; is it still true?"

Curiosity had him turning to find the verses. He read it out loud. "Love suffers long and is kind; love does not envy; love does not … "

Steve thought about the words as he read them. *I can see how my wife has put these words to practice in our life. I've sure tried her patience, but she bore it all, endured it all, and still loved me.*

He tried doing what she had written. He tried putting his own name there, but it didn't work. He couldn't truthfully say all those things about himself. He could believe it about April—but not about himself. *God, this is what she's been doing. She's been showing me the kind of love You show people. Oh, Lord, what have I done? I have been so wrong in so many ways! Can she ever forgive me? Lord, can you?*

I WAS WATCHING A MOVIE in bed with my head elevated when Mindy walked in with a bouquet of flowers and a box of chocolates. "Mindy! How are you? Thank you for the flowers. They're gorgeous!"

Mindy placed the flowers on the wide windowsill and handed me the chocolates.

"Contraband!" I remarked with a smile. "I'll need some help please." I lifted my right arm to display the cast. "My hand doesn't bend at all right now."

Mindy opened the box.

I picked out one piece and then another. "Hide it in the drawer of the table. I better not eat too many, but I really need some chocolate right now."

"Sure thing." She closed the lid and placed the box in the drawer. "How are you doing?"

"Better, but I'll be here a while. What's going on with you and Joe?"

"I'm okay. Joey's with his dad this weekend. Joe's still with 'the other woman.' I filed for divorce. He says he won't fight me, so I'll get the house and primary custody of Joey. He'll get every other weekend. It'll take a couple of months to get it all done."

"I was on my way to see you when I had my accident."

"Oh? How come?"

"I thought Steve was having an affair, and I was going to come over to talk to you. I saw Steve with a woman at a restaurant, and I thought he was with his fling. I got upset and took off. That's how I ended up at the lake and on that trail. I made a mess out of everything. The thing is that Steve did have an affair, but he'd already broken it off, and the woman I saw him with was his boss's wife. Totally innocent."

"Well, that explains the message I got from Judy. But I don't understand—if Steve had an affair, why aren't you more upset?"

"Let me begin at the beginning." I filled her in about findmysoulmate.org and everything else.

When lunch came for me, Mindy ran down to the cafeteria and got something for herself. When she returned, we visited some more. *Great girl talk. I think Mindy needed it too. I remember how I felt when the whole Cliff and Chloe thing blew up.* I was also reminded of the joys of having a girlfriend. I felt like things were coming full circle somehow, a healing in its own way.

Mindy stayed until two o'clock when June and Larry showed up. I was sad to see her go, but she promised to come again and to keep in touch. We both knew it would be a while before I got back to work.

June and Larry also had a bouquet of flowers and lots of news about the baby. They had started emptying a room and purchasing baby things. It was still early, but they planned to get one big item each month and two boxes of diapers. They'd be pretty well set by the time the baby came. They just bought a crib, a matching changing table, and a dresser. June said, "If it's a girl, we decided we'll use Mae as the middle name to honor Mom. We're still discussing first names, but that part's settled."

I replied, "So, if it's a boy, you have a first name and no middle name, and if it's a girl, you have a middle name and no first name. That sounds about right!" I smiled.

"Thanks, sis. Leave it to you to point out the obvious. And … we're getting a puppy. Just one." She held up a finger for emphasis. "We've already picked it out. It's one of Maggie's. An adorable male. You know the one. Mom named him Rambo."

"Perfect," I responded. "I'm glad you decided to do that. Now's the time for sure. It will help keep you busy while you're waiting for the baby, and you can have the training part done before the baby arrives."

"I certainly hope so," Larry said. "But I think it will be fun. What's Steve up to?"

I mentioned the dogs Steve adopted and the camping trip. We talked about Mom and her dogs. We also revisited how many times we'd been to hospitals when we were growing up. I now won the prize for more times. We said a prayer together before they left: for my healing, for Mom, for their baby, and for Steve's trip.

The food tray brought a surprise: no more liquid diet. "Soft mechanical," the nurse called it. Baby steps, I suppose, but at least I could sink my teeth into it. I didn't confess about my hidden chocolate. I was able to feed myself slowly with my left hand, and it was not as messy. When I finished, they cleared my tray.

With my head elevated, I gazed out the window and thought of what I had lost. I didn't know why I was going down that path. Maybe the visit from June. I started crying.

No more Brody. I sure will miss him. He was truly a great dog. How can I replace a dog like that? And no babies for us. I'm still not sure how I feel about that. It hurts, but I know I have to accept it. Being bitter won't do me any good, but I do have a right to mourn both losses. I decided that much and let myself cry.

Tears silently streamed down my face as Mom walked in. "Hey, baby girl, how are you?" She rushed to my bedside, nearly dropping her bouquet. She righted it and placed it next to the others on the windowsill. "Are you okay? Are you hurting? Can I get you anything?"

I patted my face with the back of my left hand. "It's okay, Mom. I was just thinking."

"Anything I can help with?" she asked.

"No. I was missing my dog and thinking about never being a mom."

She gave me a gentle hug. "I know it hurts, honey, but in Brody's case, Steve adopted two more dogs. You have honored his memory by passing on the love."

"How did you know? Oh, the shelter. Did you work there today?"

"Yes. My first full day there. It was very interesting. I walked all the dogs and spent time with them. I got to meet some of the people who came in to adopt. Cindy does the interviews. She's not the only one who can, but I'm not up to speed on everything yet. It was a good day. I enjoyed it."

"That's so awesome, Mom. I'm so glad for you. It will keep you young, you know?"

"Great. I'm about to retire, and now I get to be young again!"

We laughed, but I quickly got serious again. "Can we talk?"

She sat down by my bed. "Fire away."

"You know how I said I had some things about my marriage that troubled me?"

"Yes, dear." She paused. "June talked to me."

"Oh, well." I took a deep breath, relieved I didn't have to rehash the whole thing. "I was right. No, I was wrong. That's not right either. I mean, I was right, but I was wrong. Wow, I'm saying this all wrong!"

"I know. The woman in the restaurant versus the other woman," she said calmly.

"But I was wrong too, Mom. I went on a dating site and met a man. I didn't meet him in real life, but that was wrong too. And the whole infertility thing. How do we get past all this?"

She didn't respond at first. Of course, I had thrown a whole bunch at her. Finally, she took my hand. "First of all, whether or not you can have babies does not define who you are. I know it's hard to accept, but it's a fact you have to work through. Ask God to guide you. Let Him work that out for you."

I closed my eyes. "Okay. And I want my marriage to work. It's the forgiveness part."

"You have to give this to God too. If you hold onto this even a little bit, it will always taint your relationship. Your father never mentioned my little affair. I did a few times, and he finally said, 'You need to let that go. I did.' I was shocked by how matter-of-fact he was because it was a huge deal to me. For him, he had dealt with it. *Over. Done. Period.* It was the healthier way to handle it. If you keep revisiting a pain and picking the scab off a wound, it will never heal."

"You're right. Part of me wants to punish him. I don't want it to happen again—by either of us."

"There's no guarantee. You can only be responsible for yourself."

"Okay, I give. You're right. Jesus forgave me and can help me forgive him. And I can try to trust him."

She gave me a quick finger jab. "Bingo, sister!"

"You know, it's a lot easier to say this stuff than it is to live it."

Mom winked at me. "Spoken like a true hypocrite."

"Thanks, Mom."

"Always glad to help, dear."

Mom stayed another hour. It was a good visit.

"Better go," she finally said.

I talked her into giving me a piece of contraband chocolate before she left. She popped one in her mouth, calling it a "finder's fee." *God blessed me with a good mother. I am so grateful.*

After she left, I relaxed and thought, *A busy day. All the company made it easier not to miss Steve and wonder how he is doing.*

I prayed for him.

SUNDAY MORNING, I GOT CREAM of Wheat. I convinced them to include a dash of milk and some sugar. Yum! I also got a piece of toast. The nurse had to help me with the butter. I dipped the toast in the hot cereal. It was lukewarm, but it was still a treat after the previous meals. I knew everyone would be at church, so I didn't expect any visitors. I found a church service to watch on TV.

About ten o'clock, the physical therapist came in. Ted talked me through everything, but he made the muscles work too. I was sore when he was done, and I was glad for the rest. Ted told me I would be progressing with the PT as time passed—even with my arm in a cast. I couldn't use a walker, but I'd have to start using those muscles again.

Ted answered all my questions and made me feel like we had a plan. We were still talking when Dr. Stevens came in. She checked me over and went through my chart. "How do you feel things are going for you?"

"I feel I'm in good hands, but when do I get out of here?"

"You'll be here for several weeks. You'll be moved to the rehab floor … maybe by the end of the week. They'll get you up and going again there."

Not the news I wanted to hear, but what can I do?

AFTER LUNCH, I WAS INUNDATED with visitors. Mindy and my mom. June and Larry. Pastor Randy. Then Denise and Richard came through the door. June, Larry, and Mom got to meet them too. My room didn't clear out until suppertime. All pleasant visits.

Mom was the last to leave. "I'm so glad you've made new friends," she said. "Women friends to do girl stuff with and chat."

Moms never stop being moms, I suppose.

MIKE DIDN'T SEE STEVE ANYWHERE. He said, "Lucy, I'm going back to camp to check on things."

At camp, Duke and Ruby were both tied up, which worried him. He headed to the tent to make sure Steve was gone before he looked elsewhere. He pulled back the tent flap and saw Steve with an open Bible in his hands.

"I get it now," Steve said. "I found it. April left me the answers." He held up a bookmark and read the comments about 1 Corinthians.

Mike responded, "The love ."

"This is what I was looking for. I could see the God of judgment and retribution and all that, but I didn't see the love. I was living with it right in front of me every day, but I didn't even notice. I've been such an idiot!"

"Brother, we can all be idiots. That's why God created forgiveness, grace, and mercy. He knew we'd mess up and need help."

"I need to go see April. I have to go."

"Understood, can I help?"

They had Steve's tent packed away and all his gear wrapped up in half an hour.

"I can't thank you guys enough," Steve said.

"Sure you can. Go to church with us next week."

Steve shook his hand with a big smile. "I'd be glad to!" He untied the dogs and was about to walk off. He stopped and said, "Please tell the others I'll see them."

The dogs were happy to be on the move. He drove the pickup home, got the dogs settled in, and headed to the hospital.

STEVE ENTERED MY ROOM AT six-thirty. I was watching a movie alone. I greeted him with a big smile. "Hey! I didn't expect to see you this early!" He was carrying my Bible.

"I know, but I have something to talk to you about." He sat down next to me. "I went to Elbow Lake this weekend, to God's Elbow, and I found Him there, April. Just like you said that day we were there together. I didn't understand before. I didn't get all the God stuff you kept talking about. I saw people hurt and hurting, but I didn't see the love. I didn't see the good in any of it, but I found some stuff in here." He held up the Bible. "The verses on the Roman Road were totally awesome! I put my name where the word 'love' is. That was killer. That's when it all hit home for me.

"This God you talk about uses people to show us what He's like. He used you to show me what real love is. You *are* loving and forgiving, patient and kind. I've messed up a lot, but you still love me. That's what God does, right? He loves us even when we mess up. We just have to be honest about it. Is that it? Is that right?"

Tears flowed as I responded, "Oh, Steve, yes, that's right."

He grabbed my hand. "I have so many things I want to ask forgiveness for, April. Can you ever forgive me?"

"You know I have made plenty of my own mistakes. Shall we start clean? What's past is past. Let's move forward together. You, me, and Jesus."

"Please," he replied. "I want that. I want a new life with you."

Epilogue

Steve took me to Brody's grave when we left the hospital, and we left flowers. It was hard, but it was also a privilege to see him in that place of honor. Steve also saved the newspaper article about Brody for me.

It's hard to believe it's been three years since I took that fall. I stayed in the hospital for six weeks. Steve came to see me every day, and we read the Bible together. Sometimes we were joined by one or more of our friends or family members.

Steve accepted Christ. He went to church with Mike, Bob, my mom, or June and Larry while I was in the hospital. Once I got out, we started going back to the Christian church in town where I had been going. Steve joined the flock and was baptized within a month of my release. I can't tell you what a blessing it has been in our lives. We have had some tough times in the past few years, but they have been so much easier to handle with us both walking with God.

We lost Steve's dad, but Steve was able to reach out to this mother. She is going to church with us now. He has been talking to his sister, Karen, more. She isn't attending a church yet, but she is open—and they have great discussions. Steve says the Lord is tugging at her heart.

Ruby and Duke are awesome dogs. They love to hike and

camp with us. They don't sleep on the bed anymore, but I can tell they get up there when they're home alone.

My mom retired that September after her birthday. She still volunteers at the shelter. She met a "friend" at church. His name is Daniel. They have gone out to dinner a few times, and they like to go for walks with their dogs. Mom says it's nothing serious, and we're all good with that. She has someone to share things with, and they can move at whatever pace they want.

June and Larry have two beautiful children now. Reyna Mae is two and a half years old, and Mitchell Lawrence is sixteen months old. They are adorable. June has been trying to get pregnant again. Steve and I couldn't be more excited. This one is for us!

June offered to be our surrogate. It took a lot of praying and planning, but we decided to go for it. The in vitro stuff was a learning experience, but this baby is 100 percent MacIntyre.

Ring, ring.

Steve grabbed the phone and brought it to me. It was June. I put the phone on speaker and said, "Hello?"

"Guess what? We're pregnant!"

About the Author

Kathy started life in Sioux City, Iowa as the youngest child in a military family. Travel and new experiences were common events in her childhood. She was raised mostly in the United States. At the age of 17, she graduated high school and joined the Army. As an adult, her faith and sense of adventure has guided her in many directions. Eventually leading her to Idaho in her mid 30s where she met her husband, Greg. Greg is a source of love, support and laughter. Greg says they have half a herd of kids and a herd and a half of grandkids. Kathy has many interests and hobbies. She loves being outdoors, making specialty birthday cakes, homemade candies and breads, sewing and photography. Her photography includes the beautiful mountain scenes surrounding her as well as family portraits and weddings. Their love of animals has resulted in having two dogs, two cats and a bird that are all rescues. A running joke is that everyone in the house is a rescue, people included.

Printed in the United States
By Bookmasters